Holly Webb

SCHOLASTIC

For my parents, whose family stories I borrowed for this book – turned upside down and inside out, and probably unrecognizable, but there from the very beginning.

Scholastic Children's Books
An imprint of Scholastic Ltd
Euston House, 24 Eversholt Street, London, NW1 1DB, UK
Registered office: Westfield Road, Southam, Warwickshire, CV47 0RA
SCHOLASTIC and associated logos are trademarks and/or
registered trademarks of Scholastic Inc.

First published in the UK by Scholastic Ltd, 2018

Text copyright © Holly Webb, 2018

The right of Holly Webb to be identified as the author
of this work has been asserted by her.

ISBN 978 1407 17086 2

Printed by CPI Group (UK) Ltd, Croydon, CR0 4YY
Papers used by Scholastic Children's Books are made
from wood grown in sustainable forests.

1 3 5 7 9 10 8 6 4 2

www.scholastic.co.uk

Chapter One

The front door clanged shut behind them, and Evie stifled a sigh. It had been so good to be outside as they walked back from the church, with the sea winds blowing away the awfulness for a little while. But now the hot, dusty air of the house felt thick and stale. Even their own garden seemed fenced around with sadness. Mama and Daddy were making their way back in the carriage, with Mama in such a state of collapse that Daddy had sent the girls home with David to look after them.

"What should we do?" Kitty asked, in a thin voice. Her face looked small and pale and pinched inside all that black. It even took the blue out of her eyes, and left her fair hair whitish and flat. Evie decided that she probably looked about the same – except with a red nose, because she'd cried at the graveside and Kitty hadn't. Kitty had only stood, staring down at the coffin, which seemed to be so much smaller than Alexander had been. Perhaps it was because Alecky had felt bigger than he really was, since he was so loud and bright and everywhere. He was like that all the time – until he wasn't there any more.

"What should we do?" Kitty asked again. "Is Mama home?"

Evie looked up at her older brother. David was fifteen. He was supposed to be looking after them. He was supposed to know what to do. But he looked just as lost as she felt, flicking his head from side to side, as though he was hoping that someone would appear, someone who understood what was happening. In the end he sat down on the odd little wooden bench by the hatstand and laughed miserably. "Do you know what Alecky would have called you in that get-up?" He waved at Evie and Kitty, swathed in black from head to foot, and trailing veils from their hats. "A pair of black beetles." Then he sniffed.

"Or silly old bats," Kitty agreed, and lifted her arms to flap the strange cape-like coat that the dressmaker had run up.

Evie sniggered, and then clapped her hand over her mouth, shocked at herself. Their brother was *dead*. She shouldn't be laughing. But they'd been silent and sad and so very beautifully behaved for more than a week, and the laughter seemed to be building up inside her, blowing up like a balloon. She'd heard two old ladies in the churchyard say that she and Kitty looked like little saints, so sweetly pretty and good, and she had been delighted, and drooped her head a fraction more before catching herself at it and blushing scarlet with shame. She had been glad of the stifling black veil. It was just – it had felt like acting. As if they were playing a game, like charades. It was so hard to remember that this was real – it had all happened so fast, and since Alecky had been ill, she seemed to have been moving through the days in a dream. She kept having to run to catch up, and now everything had got ahead of her.

She fought the laughter back, and took off her black gloves. They couldn't stand around in the hallway all day. Evie realized that she had been waiting for Miss Jennings to scoop them up and tell them to run and change their shoes, and take off the hats and the bat cloaks and find their sewing, or look at that French vocabulary. She kept forgetting that Miss Jennings was gone too. Mama had sent her away.

Evie wasn't actually sure that Mama had been right about it all being Miss Jennings' fault. Alecky had been the one who went scrambling about on the rocks at Saltwick Bay, soaking his boots and stockings just as he always did. Miss Jennings had told him to stay on the sand, and only turned her back on him for a minute while Kitty was shrieking about a jellyfish. Miss Jennings had hustled them home and made Alecky change straight away. But it was the first week of July – *summer* – and it had been hot and sticky for weeks and weeks. Daddy had taken them sea bathing only the week before and Mama had said that was very good for their health. Why was it so much worse to get wet boots and stockings than it was to go bathing in the sea?

So it couldn't really be down to the governess that Alecky had caught a chill. He had crept about the house coughing for days, until one morning he was just too tired and weak to get out of bed. He died three days later, of a "galloping pneumonia". The maids said he coughed himself to death – Evie had heard Sarah and Lizzie discussing it while they were fixing black crepe over the door knocker.

Mama dismissed Miss Jennings that day, and

the girls had watched her walk silently up the stairs with her handkerchief pressed to her eyes. It had been one of the handkerchiefs that Kitty had embroidered her for Christmas, with *MJ* in the corner, because they didn't know the governess's first name, and just *J* hadn't seemed quite right. She hadn't even said goodbye to them, merely whispered something they couldn't catch and hurried into her room. An hour or so later they stood at the landing window and watched Miss Jennings carry her battered little suitcase down St Hilda's Terrace towards the station.

Evie had worried about Miss Jennings ever since. She was the nicest governess they'd had, and where was she now? She wouldn't have another family to go to, not straight away. She was probably stuck in a nasty boarding house, answering advertisements in the newspapers in her beautiful handwriting.

Evie sometimes told herself that Miss Jennings and Alecky were off somewhere together, with the governess eternally running after him, telling him to leave that stray dog alone, and stop dragging sticks along railings like a common urchin.

"We'd better go upstairs," Evie murmured to Kitty. "Mama and Daddy will be back soon." Even though their parents had the carriage, it was such a long way round to St Mary's by the road that it was actually quicker to walk. The girls and David had stood on the bridge across the harbour for a few minutes, all of them silently watching the tide as it swept out to sea. Evie looked longingly at the lighthouses marking the edge of the harbour. They were so close to the beach. Miss Jennings had taken them out almost every day, striding along the sands even if the wind was blowing them sideways. But since she'd gone, Evie and Kitty had been shut up in the house. They weren't used to going out by themselves, even though no one had actually said that they couldn't. Instead, they spent most of their time up in the faded old room that had been their nursery.

They were all too old for a nursery now, of course – even Alecky had been. But no one could think of another name for it that would stick. Most of their things were in there – the dolls' house that Evie and Kitty shared, shelves of battered dolls and their clothes. Alecky had been playing with his trains that afternoon when they'd come back from Saltwick Bay, and they were still set out all over the nursery floor. The girls had moaned at him for not tidying them away, but now no one wanted to move them. Even the maids were sweeping around the tracks, and the trains were growing a faint coating of dust.

Kitty stepped carefully into the middle of the tracks and sat down, hunching herself up and hugging her knees. She pulled out a handkerchief – it had an inch-wide black border – and gently polished the top of the nearest train, so the green and gold paint shone again. "How long do you think it will take," she asked Evie hoarsely, "before we can bear to put them away?" She swallowed, and half coughed. "I mean, before we don't care and just think that they're annoying because we keep falling over them?"

Evie shook her head. "I don't know. I suppose it'll be like that sometime. But I can't imagine when. Not for ... years maybe." The two girls stared silently at the trains. "The baby in between you and me died, did you know that?" she said at last.

Kitty stopped polishing and looked up at her in surprise. "No!"

"It was a boy. Miss Jennings told me."

Kitty sighed. "I suppose I was a terrible disappointment, then."

"They already had David," Evie pointed out. "It wasn't as if we were all girls." She picked up a train and began to wipe it with the hem of her dress. "There's a long gap between me and David too. So ... I expect that means other babies died. I'm just saying ... I suppose Mama has had this happen before." She rubbed harder at a spot of something on the dark blue paint. Probably biscuit. Or jam. It was sticky. "It's worse now, of course. Because Alecky was so much older."

"Do you think it might happen to me?" Kitty dropped her handkerchief and stared at Evie, her pale eyes widening. "I'm only a little bit older than Alecky is. I mean, he was." She caught her breath anxiously.

"It won't," Evie said hurriedly. But she wasn't really sure, and she suspected that Kitty could hear it in her voice.

"I shan't ever get my feet wet."

"I don't think it made any difference," Evie whispered. "I think it was just a thing that happened. A very bad thing." Then she looked guiltily over her shoulder, sure she had heard a scuffling, like someone just outside the door. Mama didn't often come up to the nursery, but what if she had heard them talking about the babies?

"It's only the dogs, silly," Kitty said, as a large Airedale terrier barged his way through the door to lean lovingly against Evie's shoulder. His wiry, curly fur tickled her ear, and she rubbed his nose. "Hello, Brandy angel," Evie murmured.

"Don't let Mama hear you say that," Kitty reminded her. "Not when Alecky actually *is* an angel. She'll be furious, and then she'll cry again."

Evie nodded. Yesterday, Mama had turned down an invitation for Kitty to go and play at the house next door, and Kitty had said gratefully that she'd rather die than play with Edith anyway, since she was the most frightful baby. There had been a frozen silence at the breakfast table, and then Mama had dropped a knife on her plate with a terrible sharp ring of china and fled the room with her handkerchief pressed up against her mouth. Everyone was trying to watch their words, but it was so difficult to remember everything that might be wrong. David had almost stopped talking altogether.

Brandy pulled his head away from Evie's shoulder, and looked round at the door with a patient sort of expression around his muzzle, or so Evie thought. "Come on!" Evie called. "Nearly there!"

There was a frantic scurrying, and a tiny dachshund puppy hurtled through the open door and into Evie's lap, where he collapsed, panting heavily.

"He's exhausted," Evie cooed. "Poor Max, all those stairs. Did Brandy leave you behind?"

Max had only just conquered stairs. Until a week or so before, he had always needed to be carried up, since his legs just weren't long enough to climb. Brandy had alternated between standing on the step above and uttering encouraging barks, or galloping away and leaving the tiny dog behind. Evie suspected he was still rather jealous, and he enjoyed the five or ten minutes of fussing that he got before the smaller dog caught up with him. Brandy had once tried to help by picking Max up by the scruff of his neck and carrying him up the stairs, but Max had squirmed so much he had to let go, and then the puppy bit him, quite hard, so he hadn't tried again.

The girls' father said that Brandy was in a state of armed neutrality, but then he'd stopped smiling and muttered something to David about the Balkan situation, and Evie wasn't entirely sure what he'd meant. She stroked Max's silken back, and he whined with pleasure, slumping over to show off his brownish-pink belly and wave his ginger paws at her. He was a most beautiful little dog, as glossy black as Daddy's boots, with neat ginger eyebrows and long, drooping black ears. His ears had flapped back now, trailing over Evie's skirt.

"His ears are half as long as he is," Kitty pointed out. "I expect that's another reason he's so slow on stairs, he must keep tripping over them. Silly little dog." She scratched Brandy's chin lovingly.

Max opened one eye and looked sideways at Kitty. He knew quite well that she liked Brandy more than she liked him, and he was very haughty about it.

"He'll grow into his ears," Evie said, running one of them through her fingers like warm silk. "He might even be as long as Brandy. Just with short legs."

The little dog made one of his sudden leaps, twisting himself upright and scrabbling his way off Evie's lap. He stood by the tracks, wagging his whiplike tail and sniffing at the trains while barking a series of sharp yaps.

"Don't let him eat them!" Kitty squealed. "Not Alecky's trains."

"He isn't going to. No, Max. Leave."

Max looked round at her, his black eyes reproachful. *As if I would*, he seemed to be saying. He nudged the tracks with his nose, and then delicately picked up a small wooden tree in his teeth. Evie heard it crunch as she dived to save it, and Kitty shrieked, "I told you! Bad dog! He ruins everything!"

Evie picked Max up and pulled a handful of wet splinters out of his mouth as he mock-growled at her. Kitty and Brandy gave them identical horrified looks. "It's only a tree," she muttered. "It isn't that important."

"What would Alecky have said?" Kitty shook her head woefully. "He loved those trains, and all the trees and houses. He would have been furious." She lowered her eyelashes and glanced slyly through them at Evie. "I ought to tell Mama."

"You wouldn't?" Evie stared at her.

"Well, maybe I wouldn't," Kitty agreed cheerfully. "But next time we're in trouble for something, *you* have to own up. He's *your* dog."

"I suppose." Evie sighed.

"And you have to do what I say for the next thirty-seven minutes exactly."

Kitty had been given a tiny carriage clock for her birthday, a few days before Alecky had been taken ill, and she adored it and carried it around everywhere. She particularly adored Evie not having one, and took every opportunity to rub it in. Evie didn't care. Max had been her birthday present, and she much preferred him to a clock, even if he did eat everything he could reach.

"Why thirty-seven minutes?" she asked.

"Just because. Come on." Kitty picked up her clock by its little silver handle and paraded it out of the room, with Evie and the two dogs trotting after her along the passage to the bedroom they shared.

Evie sighed as Kitty reached up to open their wardrobe. She knew exactly what they would be doing for the next thirty-seven minutes, and she was sick of it. "We shouldn't change out of our blacks," she pointed out. "No one told us to."

"It doesn't matter if we're going to put them back on again," Kitty said. "Or we can just put the tunics on over the top. Please, Evie, please. . ." She widened her eyes hopefully, and then gave Max a meaningful glance. There were still tiny pieces of green painted wood around his muzzle.

Evie reached in and lifted down two hangers

with dark wool tunics on, and gold cord sashes draped around the hooks. Kitty gave a gleeful gasp as Evie handed her the smaller tunic. She held it up against her front, twirling a little in front of the mirror in the wardrobe door. "Don't you dare!" she snapped, as Max lunged for the tasselled end of the sash. She snatched it out of his way, and the dachshund slunk back crossly and crawled under Evie's bed to sulk.

The tunics had arrived from the outfitters the day before, and Kitty was in love with them. Not just the way they made her and Evie look so smart and schoolgirlish, but what they *meant*. No more Miss Jennings (Kitty didn't miss her nearly as much as Evie did, partly because Miss Jennings had been unjustly critical of Kitty's spelling). Instead, Daddy had come home from his office and told them that they were going to school. David had been at boarding school for years, of course, and Alecky would have gone away in a year's time, but no one had ever suggested that Evie and Kitty should go.

Mama liked them being educated at home. But Daddy had met one of the governors of the new school up at the top of Prospect Hill, and said that the place sounded just the thing. He had written to the headmaster to enrol them both, since the school now had a preparatory department for Kitty too. He had even sent to Spanton's for the tunics and blouses the girls were to wear, and the sashes that showed that they were in Gold set. They would start in the new term, in September.

Evie and Kitty had read the prospectus over and over, wondering what it would be like to go to school. It was only a thin leaflet, with no pictures, but they had seen other children going to the County School when they were out with Miss Jennings, and envied the girls in their smart outfits, and the laughing, gossiping groups as they hurried up the hill from the town. The uniform meant they wouldn't have to wear black, too, at least not all the time. Six months of black dresses, it should have been, for a brother.

"You might have to work harder, you know," Evie warned Kitty now. "I expect they'll be just as fussy about spelling as Miss Jennings was."

"*Nobody* could be," Kitty said, twisting the sash round her fingers. "For a start, there'll be lots of other girls, and boys even, in the prep class. So the teacher won't be looking at only *my* spelling, will she?" She looked up at Evie, her smile fading a little. "Do you think Mama will take us to the school?"

Evie frowned. The way Mama was at the moment – quite usual one minute, and then in floods of tears the next – it could be rather embarrassing if she insisted on coming, even if it was only to the gate. "No. . ." she said thoughtfully. "She didn't want us to go to school, I think she wanted us to have another governess. So I shouldn't think she'll walk us there." Evie had heard them arguing about it yesterday, when the uniform had arrived from the outfitters. Mama had accused Daddy of trying to take all her babies away from her. She had been shrieking, and Evie had whirled around and hurried Kitty back upstairs.

"We can go by ourselves," Kitty said stoutly, though she looked a little worried. "All the others do. Some of them go on the bus, even, I've seen them." Her eyes widened. "Imagine, going on a bus, all on your own."

Evie nodded. "I expect we'll get used to that sort of thing," she murmured. It was going to be very different from being shepherded everywhere by Miss Jennings. "Here, let me put that over your head." She dropped the boxy tunic over Kitty's black dress, and tied the sash for her. The tunic was rather long, even with the sash to haul it up. It came practically to Kitty's ankles, and Evie eyed it worriedly. Miss Jennings or Mama had always seen to their clothes before. Things that didn't fit were whisked away to be altered by someone Mama knew from church, who took in sewing. She had made them the odd bat coats. Evie didn't think that asking Mama about the tunics would be a good idea, not now. But anyway, there were weeks before they were to start school. Perhaps Kitty would grow. Or Mama would be ... different. Evie looked at Kitty, so little and absurd in her dress and tunic and sash, like a suet pudding all tied up with string, and a flare of furious sisterly love burned up inside her. It was only her and Kitty now. Alecky was gone, and David was too old to count, or to count on. Kitty was not going to suffer, Evie would not allow it. If anyone at the school dared to tease her about the tunic, she would – she would – but exactly *what* she would do Evie didn't know yet. Her sole experience of school was from a parcel of Angela Brazil stories that their aunt had sent her. Evie had read them over and over, fascinated, wondering if this was really what school was like.

The surge of love died down, and Evie felt the awful strangeness rush in to fill the hole it had left behind. It was so very odd to know that Alecky would not be coming back. The wrongness of it didn't seem to be going away, the way it had when

Peter, her rabbit, had died. Evie had cried and cried for days, but then she'd forgotten, except when she walked by his empty hutch, and even then it was only duty tears. After that it had been her birthday, and Daddy had given her Max.

Of course it was wrong to think that you could replace a brother like you had replaced a rabbit, but somehow Evie had thought that was what would happen. Instead the aching hole inside her kept emptying out and gaping, and stupid things like the model trains and Brandy scratching at Alecky's bedroom door made her want to howl.

"Take it off now, Kitty, do," she said, sharply enough to make Brandy's ears twitch. "What if Mama does come up here, or sends one of the maids? You'll get into trouble." She caught the end of Kitty's sash and tugged, and her little sister reluctantly drew away from the mirror. "I suppose you're right," she sighed. "I wish it was September now." She submitted to being peeled out of the school tunic, and watched Evie hang it up again. Then she opened the drawer in her chest to admire the cream shantung blouses she was to wear under it, so perfectly clean and folded. She sat down on the floor, put her arm around Brandy, and opened up the green leather cover of her little travelling clock. "It hasn't been thirty-seven minutes, nor anywhere near," she muttered stubbornly.

"Well, what do you want to do for the next however-long-it-is?" Evie asked, sitting down opposite and lifting Max into her lap while trying hard to remember that sense of sisterly love that had blazed inside her a moment before.

Kitty stared at her, and then sniffed, and as Evie watched, her eyes seemed to fill up and overflow, like Kitty herself pouring barley water into a glass. The tears streamed down her face. "I don't know," she whispered haltingly, as Brandy licked at her with worried little whines. "Nothing's good. I don't know what to do."

Evie scooted her way across the floor to cuddle her sister and the dogs close. "Me either. I don't think anyone does, Kitty." Then she flinched. "Someone *is* coming!" She glanced worriedly towards the wardrobe to make sure they had put the school tunics away properly, and scrambled up, yanking Kitty after her, and brushing the dusty skirts of her little sister's dress.

"Evie! Kitty! Where are you?" The door crashed open, and David stood there panting. He had raced up the stairs, Evie thought, wondering if Mama had heard. "Ssshhh!" She flapped her hands at him. "Remember Mama! The funeral! Ssshhh!"

"No, no." David grabbed her arm, squeezing so hard she almost squeaked. "You don't understand, Evie, listen. Father's back—"

"Well then, Mama must be too, so do be quiet, Davy, please, and let me *go*—"

But David only gripped her harder, giving her arm a little shake. "Father brought Mama home in the carriage ages ago, and he went to the office, *listen*! Germany has invaded Belgium! Mr Asquith has made a speech in the House, we have sent Germany an ultimatum!"

"A what?" Kitty put in, and David blinked at her. Evie took the chance to pull away, rubbing her arm and glaring at her brother as he tried to explain. "Oh. . . An ultimatum. Umm. As if we were saying, *Do as you're told, or else*. They are at war with France, you see, and Russia, but we were holding back. We can't do that now, because we promised ages ago to defend Belgium. Now that Belgium has been invaded, we *must* protect them – we're sworn to. Father says that the king has called up all the reservists. Apparently York is full of men rushing to join the army!"

"Is Mr Asquith that man with the pince-nez glasses who lives further up the hill?" Kitty asked thoughtfully. "I thought his name was Aston."

"Kitty! No! Mr Asquith is the prime minister," David hissed. "Don't either of you see? We're going to war with Germany!"

Evie stared at him, and then shook her head doubtfully. "No . . . that can't be right. This is all because that duke was shot, isn't it? That was so far away, Davy, it can't be anything to do with us. Not when he was shot in Serbia. I hadn't even heard of Serbia until Daddy started talking about it at breakfast."

"It is. You'll see." David slumped down on Kitty's bed, shaking his head. "I wonder what it means for all of us. . . Perhaps they won't send me back to school. I wouldn't even be surprised if the school was closed."

"No school!" Kitty yelped. "Why not?"

"Yes, why not?" Evie bit her lip. All their thinking and planning, and now it would be for nothing. "I don't see why schools should close. That's nonsense!"

David shrugged. "Oh well, maybe not. But our school has an Officers' Training Corps. I was just thinking that perhaps we'd all be called up. I forgot about the lower forms."

"But you're only fifteen." Evie frowned. "Even you couldn't be sent to fight. Could you?"

"I don't see why not!" David exclaimed, sitting up suddenly. "We're trained."

"Do you want to?" Evie asked curiously.

"Of course I do. We have to protect Belgium, Evie. The Germans have behaved dreadfully." David's voice was earnest, and he was banging his fist into Kitty's bedspread, so that it bounced and slumped with every blow. Evie didn't think he realized that he was doing it. "They're being absolute thugs. Everyone says so, all the chaps at school. One of our masters was telling us only last term that a war was bound to happen sooner or later, because Germany wants to make the whole of Central Europe into a Teutonic state – that means German," he added, before Kitty could ask.

"Like the Empire?" Evie frowned.

"Exactly." David nodded, his eyes blazing with the horror of it. "If we do go to war – and I'm sure we will, it's a matter of our honour – we'll have the whole thing wrapped up by Christmas."

"Because we're much better than the Germans," Kitty said confidently, and David smiled at her, a rather patronizing little smile. "Of course."

Would they all have forgotten Alecky by Christmas too, Evie wondered, watching David's eager face as he talked on and on about what the masters at school had said, and what their father had said, and what the boy next door (slightly older) had said. The excitement was practically bursting out of him, and the strange, lost look he'd had as they stood in the churchyard had gone completely. Even Kitty, who was next in age to Alecky and had spent most time with him, seemed to have forgotten suddenly that they were sad. She was rooting in a toy chest at the end of her bed, searching for a packet of paper flags that Daddy had bought her to decorate sandcastles.

"There! I found it!" she squeaked delightedly,

dragging it out from underneath a stack of battered penny papers. "I knew I hadn't used the Union Jack." She pulled out the crumpled little flag and went dancing around their bedroom, waving it in wild sweeps. "God save the king! Hurrah for England! We're going to war!"

Chapter Two

After all the excitement on that Tuesday, and the formal declaration of war that night, nothing very much seemed to happen. Evie wasn't quite sure what she had *expected* to happen, but a war seemed so very important, and big. Surely it should have had more effect on their lives than just Daddy muttering at the newspaper more than usual?

The British Expeditionary Force were sent to France at once, to stand in the way of the German advance on Paris. Evie had imagined that the British soldiers would drive the Germans back easily, but it didn't seem to be happening that way. The BEF were highly trained expert marksmen, but they were hopelessly outnumbered by the German army – and they were retreating, or that was what Evie had gathered from Daddy's growling from behind the paper.

David had gone back to school, still half hoping that the training he'd had there would mean he could be called up, like all the reserve forces had been. The government was calling for volunteers, and thousands of men were enlisting every day, but it seemed that fifteen was just too young.

Kitty had forgotten about her little paper flag in the excitement of a school satchel that Daddy had brought home for her, which at present was completely empty, even though today was their first day. Neither of them was quite sure what went in satchels, but Kitty was desperate to be a schoolgirl. Evie had woken up the night before to find the wardrobe door open, and her little sister half asleep with her head pillowed on her crumpled school tunic. It was still a little long, but Evie had begged Sarah, the parlour maid, to alter it to fit properly.

Sarah had looked at her sideways, but she had agreed in the end. Evie had stumblingly offered to pay her out of their pocket money, and that seemed to have helped.

"Are you right in t'head, Miss?" Sarah had snapped. "Of course I don't need paying. Though it certainly isn't my job to alter tha clothes. Whatever tha mother got rid of that Miss Jennings for, I don't know."

"I think Mama was just … upset…" Evie faltered. "About … everything."

"Yes, well, us all are. Poor little mite." Sarah sighed heavily. "Oh, go and fetch it, Miss. And tha sister, I'd better see where it needs taking in. Does tha's fit?"

"Yes, oh, yes, beautifully." Evie nodded eagerly. "Thank you so much, Sarah."

Sarah's reaction to Kitty in her tunic had been,

"Good grief," and the cook had clearly been horrified. Evie had heard them muttering to each other as they crawled around Kitty, pinning and tacking. "Whatever's their ma thinking of?" came several times.

Evie could have told them quite easily, if she weren't pretending not to hear. Whatever their mother was thinking of wasn't Kitty and Evie. At all.

"Still in retreat," her father muttered now, shaking the paper aggressively.

"What did you say?" their mother asked, looking up vaguely. She wasn't eating, but she had a cup of tea in front of her. Evie had poured it herself.

Their father looked round his paper and smiled, lines appearing at the corners of his eyes. "The war news, darling. Not too good. Still in retreat after the battle at Mons, but fighting a brave rearguard action."

"Oh. . ."

"Daddy. . ." Evie put in quietly. "Should we leave for school, do you think?"

At this, Kitty half jumped out of her seat – she hadn't eaten anything because she was too excited, and she had fed all her toast to Brandy under the table. Then she sat down again hurriedly, not wanting to draw attention to herself. Both girls were still finding it hard to believe that they would really be allowed to go to school, even though Daddy had told them that he had paid the fees.

Not being sure that school would actually happen had meant that Evie wasn't nervous. Or not very nervous, until now, when suddenly her heart seemed to be trying to climb out of her mouth. Her hands were so cold that she buried them between her knees, pressed in the folds of her navy tunic. But their father only pulled his watch out of his waistcoat pocket and eyed it lazily. "Yes, indeed." Then he frowned, obviously remembering that they no longer had Miss Jennings to shepherd his daughters around. "Do you know the way, Evie?"

"Yes." Evie nodded eagerly. "We can walk

through the market gardens, I asked Cook and Sarah."

"Ah." Daddy was silent, and Evie wondered if she'd done something wrong by talking about all this with the servants. But he was far too busy to ask, and Mama was still so tired, and – and not there, somehow. What should she have done? At last her father nodded and said, "Good. Well done. Off you go, then. Kiss your mother goodbye, girls. Look after Kitty, won't you? Make sure she goes to the right schoolroom and such..." He stared at them, and combed his moustache with his fingers, as though he was nervous too, though Evie couldn't think why. She darted around the table and hugged him quickly, rubbing her cheek against the bristles of his moustache. "Thank you for letting us go," she whispered. "We'll be so good, I promise."

"Come on, come on," Kitty hissed from the door. She was already wearing her coat and clutching two straw hats and her satchel, and she was hopping from foot to foot with suppressed excitement. As Evie hurried out of the dining room, Kitty scrambled to open the front door, and the pair of them pattered down the steps and through the steep front garden to the road. St Hilda's Terrace stood at the very top of a hill above the town, and the best way to the school, Cook had decided, was to cut through the market gardens and nurseries that ran down the slope below them, and then go back up Prospect Hill. Kitty peered into her satchel as Evie opened the gate. "We've only got twenty minutes!"

"You're not bringing your clock?" Evie said, staring at her. She must have slipped it in there on the way down to breakfast.

"Of course! How else will I know what time it is?" Kitty shook her head, as though she thought Evie was sadly lacking.

"But what if you lose it? Or it gets broken?"

"I won't," Kitty said, with supreme confidence. "It's safe in my satchel. I'll keep it there. It's wrapped in a scarf, Evie, don't fuss."

Evie wished for Miss Jenkins all over again. She would have known how to make Kitty see sense. But Kitty was right, they couldn't risk being late on their first morning. She gave a frustrated little hiss, grabbed Kitty's hand and towed her up the road.

As they came out of the track through the nursery gardens, Evie spotted a few more girls in the County School straw hats, and several boys wearing the school tie, too. The girls' and boys' parts of the school were separate – only Kitty's junior class would be mixed – but Evie thought she recognized one of the boys who hurried past them from the ballroom dancing class Miss Jennings had accompanied them to. She didn't quite dare to speak to him, though. What if she was wrong, or some of the other girls heard her? Miss Jennings had always been very strict about the way properly brought-up girls behaved. She would have called it shockingly bad manners to speak to a strange boy. Evie stared down at her shoes instead, hardly hearing Kitty's excited chatter about how many people were making their way up the hill to the school.

"Look at those big girls!" Kitty whispered, as three older girls walked by on the other side of the road. "That girl with the dark hair is as tall as Daddy!"

"Maybe they're prefects?" Evie whispered back.

"Do you think this school *has* prefects?"

"I should think so," Evie said doubtfully. "All the schools in our books have them."

Kitty had read several of Evie's school stories as well, and she nodded. "I suppose we'll do all the things those girls in the books do. Play hockey and tennis, and have dances. It's such a pity it's not a boarding school like David's, I'd love to have a midnight feast. Oh, Evie, look, they're crossing the road!"

The three older girls were indeed crossing over, and looking curiously at Evie and Kitty. The tall dark-haired one smiled at them both and asked,

"Hello! Are you new this term?"

Kitty and Evie stared back at her, struck silent with shyness, until Evie managed to whisper, "Yes."

"What are you called?"

"Evie and Kitty Maitland."

A fair girl with a freckled nose smiled at Evie encouragingly. "I'm Leila, and this is Ailsa. Ailsa is the school captain, she's a very grand person."

Evie nodded – she had been right about the tall dark girl, if a school captain was like a prefect.

"And I'm Elaine. Have you been at school before?" the other girl put in.

Evie shook her head. "No, we had a governess. But then Daddy heard about the County School." She couldn't explain about Alecky, she thought, not without going all wobbly-voiced again. "One of the governors lives close to us."

The dark-haired girl nodded. "You have a lovely walk to school. We saw you coming down past the orchard."

"But you'll need galoshes later on in the term, it's

a sea of mud up there," Elaine pointed out. "We'd better get on, by the way, we've got the steep part to go, and it would be a bit shameful if Ailsa was late."

The tall girl rolled her eyes. "They won't stop teasing me about it," she explained to Kitty and Evie. "I've only just been chosen, and they think it's very funny, even though they're prefects too. Are you two walking on your own, even though it's your first morning? You're very brave."

"Daddy had to go to his office," Kitty said chattily, and Evie gave her an envious look. Wasn't she shy at all? "And Mama—" Then she stopped and looked anxiously at Evie. What should they say?

"She isn't very well," Evie said hurriedly.

"Never mind, we'll make sure you get to the right place. Do you know what form you'll be in?" Ailsa asked Evie. "Your sister will be in Prep, I can see that."

"I'm eleven," Evie told her. "I'm not sure." She bit her bottom lip worriedly.

"I expect you'll be in the Lower Third, unless you happen to be a genius," Elsa explained. "They'll be glad to have you, there's only eight of them just now. They're the smallest form in the school, and they don't like it."

Evie nodded. Only eight! That didn't sound too bad. In the moments when she'd allowed herself to believe that Mama wouldn't suddenly decide they must have another governess and they'd really go to school, she had wondered how she would ever remember everyone's names. There were a few other children who lived close by – silly little Edith in the next house, for one – and they had friends that they saw at church, and played with on the beach sometimes, but she had never been surrounded by a crowd of other girls.

"I suppose if you've had a governess you've never played hockey or netball?" Elaine asked. "We could do with some strong netball players for the junior team."

Evie shook her head. She was beginning to

feel as though she didn't know anything. What if she spent all her time at school being absolutely useless? She could only hope that she wouldn't turn out to be stupid as well. She was a much better speller than Kitty, but that wasn't saying much, and her piano playing was awful.

"But Evie's ever such a fast runner," Kitty said. "She wouldn't say because she's too shy, but she is. I expect she'd be very good at hockey."

"Kitty, ssshhh!" Evie flushed scarlet.

"Don't shush her," Elaine said, laughing. "It's nice that she wants to stick up for you. We've got so many sisters at the school who spend all their time squabbling. And the ones with brothers here are even worse."

"Our big brother's at a boarding school. And – oh. . ." Kitty faltered to a stop. She had obviously been about to say that Alecky was too young for school, and now the older girls were staring at them curiously.

Evie squeezed Kitty's hand and swallowed. "Our

little brother died, in July. He had pneumonia." She waved vaguely at the black band around her coat sleeve.

"I'm not surprised your mother isn't well," Ailsa said gently. "Poor you."

"Perhaps school will be a change exactly when you needed it," Elaine suggested. "And we're here, just in time. We go in here, you see, and the boys' entrance is at the other end." The big girls shepherded Evie and Kitty through a side door, and they looked around eagerly. Evie had a confused impression of one immensely long passageway, with noticeboards all along the walls and so many doors. But the strangest thing was that it was full of girls, chattering in whispers and laughing and all hurrying every which way. Everyone seemed to know exactly where they were going, and Evie hung back by the door. She wanted to be part of that crowd – she even looked almost the same, in her uniform – but the rush and noise was daunting.

"Oh, Miss Douthett!" Ailsa caught the eye of a woman wearing a smart jersey suit and yards of curiously carved wooden beads around her neck. "These are Evie and Kitty Maitland, they're new. Shall I take them to Miss Davidson's room?"

"Good morning, girls." The teacher smiled at them. "Thank you, Ailsa, you needn't worry. I have a list of the new pupils, and these are my last two. Kitty needs to go to the Prep class, and Evie will be in Lower Third. Which means I'll be your form mistress, Evie – I look after all the Thirds together. I teach art for the whole school as well."

Evie managed to smile and nod, and it was almost a real smile. She liked Miss Douthett's beads, and drawing was the one thing Miss Jennings had always praised her for. She hadn't expected that there would be a teacher just for art.

Miss Douthett led them along the passage to take Kitty into her class, which was already full of girls and boys around her age and a little younger. It was a bright room, with tall windows streaming sunlight, and Kitty smiled happily at the young teacher who welcomed her in. She hurried to sit at her new desk and winked at Evie.

Miss Douthett laughed, and beckoned Evie to follow her. "I don't think your little sister is going to take long to settle in. You haven't been to school before, have you? Your father explained to Miss Davidson."

Evie shook her head, grateful that she didn't have to tell her story all over again. "Never," she murmured.

"I'm sure you'll enjoy it. You can always come and ask me if something isn't going right. Just come along to the art room."

"A whole room? For art?" Evie looked up at her hopefully, and Miss Douthett smiled.

"Absolutely. And we have a great many plaster casts of statues, and other beautiful things to draw. We're very lucky – you'll see later on, Evie, you've an art lesson this afternoon, I believe."

"I love drawing," Evie told her. "I draw with my brother sometimes. He's determined to go to an art school when he's old enough, and he lets me use his things. He gave me a sketchbook for my birthday, and some chalk pencils."

"You'll be able to use all sorts of different materials here," Miss Douthett assured her. "Now, here we are, this is the Third Form classroom."

Even though there were only eight girls in the Lower Third, there were twelve in the Upper, so the room seemed full to bursting when Evie crept in after the form mistress. Her burst of chattiness had completely dried up, and she only just managed a faint smile when the girls at the desks next to her said hello.

"You're lucky enough to have new girls in both third forms this term," Miss Douthett explained, nodding to a rather worried-looking girl with dark curly hair. "Please do your best to look after Hilda and Evie, and make sure they know where everything is. You can catch up on your holiday news for five minutes, girls, until we go to assembly."

The five minutes' rest seemed to Evie to be the last time she caught breath for the next few hours. Even though she was surrounded by the other girls in her form, telling her their names and asking her all sorts of questions, she was at least in one place. As soon as the bell rang for assembly, she seemed to be scooped up and raced all round the building, from assembly, to fetching exercise books, to a drill class (which was dreadful, because she had no idea what any of the instructions meant, and seemed to be permanently three steps behind everyone else) and then to dinner. Even then she was forced to bolt down her food, as Sybil and Grace, the two girls who had specially adopted her, were determined that they should all attend a meeting about a folk-dancing society. After the disastrous drill, Evie wasn't sure folk dancing was a good idea, but she hated the thought of being abandoned by Sybil and Grace more.

She arrived in the afternoon's art lesson feeling as though she'd been blown through the day by a small hurricane, and it was a relief to be presented with a plain piece of paper and an arrangement of dried flowers and a Chinese fan.

"I hate drawing still life," Grace sighed, picking pieces out of her rubber. "It never goes right, and Miss Douthett laughs at me – she does!" she added indignantly as Sybil snorted at her. "I know she doesn't actually make a noise, but I can tell she's silently laughing. Art is my worst thing."

"Are you any good, Evie?" Sybil asked. "Grace's quite right, she's rotten at it."

"Thank you very much!" Grace tried to sound cross, but she was giggling. "I'll remember that next time you beg for help with your Latin prep!"

"I don't think I'm very good, but I do love drawing," Evie admitted. "Sometimes I take a little sketchbook out with me when I walk my dogs, but they're not very good at sitting still, so I never get long."

"Dogs? Of your own? Lucky!" Sybil looked interested.

"Brandy is Daddy's, he's an Airedale, but Max is just mine. I got him for my birthday, he's a dachshund pup – He's a darling."

"Gorgeous," Sybil sighed. "I suppose we ought to get on and draw, Miss Douthett's watching." She peered at her paper and held up her pencil to measure the length of the fan, while Grace drew her first line, and then growled and rubbed it out again.

"Wow, you are good!" Grace said admiringly a few minutes later, startling Evie into a little jump. "Oh! I didn't make you spoil it, did I?"

Evie smiled at her. "No, look." She quickly rubbed out the scratchy line she'd drawn, and held up the sheet of paper. "It doesn't show."

"I didn't mean to make you jump. Look, Sybil, isn't she good?"

"That's very nice, Evie. Keep on and finish it. Sybil, Grace, I'm glad to see you're encouraging Evie, but do you think you could manage some work as well?" Miss Douthett wandered off to look at the other tables, and Grace sighed.

"I don't know how she does that. She has the most silent feet I ever saw. Oh, you know what I mean. Anyway, she's going to be disappointed if I do work more on this; it's only going to get worse. Miss Douthett says I've got no sense of perspective, and she does keep trying to show me, but I don't ever seem to understand what she means." Grace wrinkled up her nose, and drew one or two vaguely flower-shaped things to show willing. "You're good enough to talk and draw at the same time, Evie. Tell us something interesting about you."

Evie opened her mouth like a fish, and gaped. "What sort of something?" she asked feebly.

"Anything!"

"I live on St Hilda's Terrace," Evie said slowly, trying to think.

"Oh, that's where." Grace peered at her drawing sadly. "I've seen you at church, so I thought you must live somewhere close to me."

"I've got a sister in the junior class?"

"Not interesting. And anyway, we know. Saw

her at dinner and she looks exactly like you only smaller." Grace set to work with her rubber again, muttering crossly.

"I'm very uninteresting," Evie said, smiling to herself as she shaded in the handle of the Chinese fan. "What about you two? Do you have sisters and brothers?"

Grace was silent a moment. "My older brother's joined up," she said at last, laying her pencil down.

Evie turned to look at her in surprise. "Already?"

"It was after the Battle of Mons was in the newspaper," Grace explained. "He bought the paper on his way to work, and he went out at dinner time and went to the recruiting office. He said he couldn't bear to read about the BEF fighting so bravely and not be part of it. He's in the Second Battalion of the Yorkshire Regiment, although he's only at a training camp now."

"All my brothers are younger than me," Sybil said regretfully. "But my sister has gone to London to stay with my aunt and join the Women's

Emergency Corps. She's working in a hostel for Belgian war refugees. She says it's good because she's actually using all the French she learned at school, but she's mostly washing up. My father hates it, because a lot of the ladies she works with are suffragettes, or they were. He thinks they're a dreadful influence on Marjorie."

"My brother wants to join the army too," Evie said. "He's only fifteen, but he keeps writing home to my father saying can't he leave school and join up."

"I wonder if we'll do anything for the war effort at school?" Sybil suggested.

"What do you mean?" Evie asked curiously. "I know there are Belgian refugees staying in Whitby too, but I'm not sure what we could do about it."

Sybil gave her a thoughtful, sideways look and then glanced at Grace, who nodded. Evie went pink. She had obviously said something rather stupid.

"I – I mean, I'd *like* to. . ." she murmured. "But I don't know how. . ."

"It's not your fault, Evie," Grace murmured comfortingly. "Sybs and I were just polishing our halos, that's all. Patting each other on the back for being lucky enough to be sent to school when we were tinies."

Evie gazed at them, feeling even more uncertain. She wasn't actually sure they were making sense at all.

Sybil smiled at her. "We mean, girls who go to school—" She broke off and looked at Grace, wrinkling her nose. "I can't think of a *nice* way to put it," she complained.

"I know. . . It's that we're expected to do things, Evie. No one runs around after us the way a mother or a governess does. And if we want to do something for the war effort, we jolly well will!"

Evie went even pinker. "You make me sound like some sort of jellyfish." After all her worrying and fussing about Kitty, and the uniform, and how to get to school, it did seem a little unfair. She stared down at her drawing and tried not to sniff. The tops of her ears burned. Sybil and Grace were right, she thought to herself. All she had really done was ask Sarah and Cook for help. How utterly feeble.

"You're not *crying*, are you?" Sybil asked. Evie couldn't tell if she was worried that they might get into trouble for upsetting a new girl, or worried that Evie was a crybaby. Possibly both.

"No!" She sat up straighter and fixed a determined look on her face. "Of course not. I think we definitely should do something for the war effort. So what shall we do?"

The answer was to form the Lower Third War Aid Committee, according to Sybil, who said that committees were official, and her sister belonged to several. It started off just as Sybil, Grace and Evie, but with quite a lot of whispering and Grace throwing her rubber at people's heads when Miss Douthett wasn't watching, by halfway through history, their last class of the day, the whole of the Lower Third had joined. Dorothea Morgan suggested asking the Uppers as well, but she was swiftly voted down. As they were packing their satchels at the end of the day, Grace explained to Evie that the Upper Thirds were a set of stuck-up little madams, and they didn't want them along.

"They'd spoil everything," Sybil agreed. "Don't be silly, Dot."

"I only thought—" Dorothea began indignantly.

"Don't. You aren't good at it."

"Oh!" Dorothea squeaked furiously, and then she glared at Evie, who hadn't been able to stop herself laughing.

"Sorry," Evie gasped.

"You can't be cross with her, Dot," Grace said soothingly. "She's new, and she's never been at school before. Let's think about what we can do."

"We can't, I have to run for my bus," Sybil said, looking anxiously up at the clock. She'd explained to Evie earlier on that she lived in a village on the moors, quite a long way out of Whitby. If she didn't catch her usual bus, there wouldn't be another for ages. Quite a few of the pupils at the County School made long journeys in from the villages. "We'll all come back with ideas tomorrow. Bye, Grace! Bye, Evie, see you in the morning!" And she dashed out of the classroom, leaving Evie staring after her with a surprised smile, and feeling as though she almost belonged.

Chapter Three

The War Aid Committee started with knitting. It wasn't very exciting, but as Sybil said, it would do until they'd thought of something better. Grace and Evie, who had more time as they lived right in the town and didn't have to catch a bus or train to school, collected pennies from the others and went to a shop in Flowergate that sold knitting wool. Evie had been there before with Mama, and remembered a huge display of fancy wools in all shades, pinks and pale blues, and masses of white wool for baby knitting. All that had been tucked away now, and the wools on the shelves were drab greys and olive green and navy.

"I don't think I'd like a muffler in any of those colours," Kitty whispered, looking at them doubtfully.

"They have to match with the uniform," Evie pointed out. "Besides, if we knitted a bright red muffler for a soldier at the front it would make him easier to see, wouldn't it? Snipers! It could be your fault that he was shot," she added.

Kitty looked suitably impressed. "Can I join your War Aid Committee?" she asked. "I can knit, almost. Or at least I can if someone else casts on."

Evie glanced anxiously at Grace. She wasn't sure what the rules were – after all, they had said no to the Upper Thirds – but surely the more knitting that was done the better.

Grace had been turning over paper patterns on the counter, all illustrated with tall, moustached soldiers swathed in thick mufflers, and odd-looking knitted helmets. "You can be an honorary member," she told Kitty. "That's very special," she added quickly, as Kitty opened her mouth to complain. "This is only twopence," she said, holding up *Field and Hospital Comforts in Knitting & Crochet.* "Do you think we should buy it? It's got lots of patterns in. Look, Rifleman's Mittens." She passed the booklet to Evie, and Kitty peered over her arm.

"What makes them for riflemen?" Evie frowned at the picture. "Oh." She shivered a little as she realized – the mittens had a separate thumb, like the ones Mama had knitted for her and Kitty, but also a separate forefinger, and both were left open, neatly ribbed around the top, so that the soldier could easily pull the trigger on his rifle. It was strange to think of something she might knit being so close to a gun.

"Is that for a *horse*?" Kitty asked, reaching over to turn the pages. "Can I make one of those? Oh, it's crochet. Could you teach me how to crochet, Evie?"

"I can't either. What is it, anyway? What's a wither, that it needs pads?"

"Evie!" Kitty looked delighted at knowing something her big sister didn't. "It's the bit just in front of where a saddle goes. I expect the pad's to stop the saddle rubbing. And I shall ask Mama to teach me to crochet. Just think of all those beautiful horses being grateful to me."

Evie rolled her eyes at Grace. "We'd better buy it. I expect we could copy out the patterns, if we buy just one." She looked rather guiltily at the clerk behind the counter, serving an elderly woman buying navy-blue wool.

"Of course we can!" Grace nodded firmly. "It's for the war effort. And anyway, just a muffler doesn't really need a pattern. This is for when we're in practice."

"Yes, miss?" The girl serving had parcelled up the navy wool now, and she turned to Grace.

"We'd like this, please, and as much wool as we can buy with sevenpence. In service colours, of course," she added rather grandly.

They walked out of the shop with a neat brown

paper parcel tucked into Grace's satchel, though Evie felt she'd quite like to carry the skeins of wool unwrapped, to show everyone that they were doing something.

By the half-term holiday, six weeks later, the WAC had gathered two completed mufflers, a sock (Dot was having trouble with turning the heel of its pair, and had undone it twice), three pairs of mittens and several knitted squares from odds and ends of wool they'd scrounged that were going to be a blanket. Kitty had started her wither pad, but was arguing to be allowed to make it in stripes, because it was going to be under a saddle anyway so it didn't matter if it was in rainbow colours.

The Upper Thirds had started their own war effort, called the Patriotic War Society, which the Lowers sneered at as blatant copying. The older girls had managed to score by finding a pattern for knitted belts, which were supposed to keep the stomach warm and prevent against cholera, besides being quite easy to make. Evie wasn't quite sure what cholera was, except that it was obviously bad, but cholera belts sounded very impressive.

"I'll finish this horrible sock over the half-term," Dot promised as they packed away their knitting to get ready for their last afternoon of lessons. "My grandmother's coming to visit, she's very good at knitting, she can help. I still don't know how I managed the first one, it must have been beginner's luck."

"I'll make more squares," Evie suggested. "Once we've sewn the blanket together, that will make quite a big parcel, don't you think? We can take it to the Red Cross depot. We could all go."

"And we have to write messages to put in all the things," Sybil said. "No, I mean it. *Good luck*, and *Keep warm, we're thinking of you*. It's what you're supposed to do. When I went to my mother's knitting circle, they all put notes in."

Grace snorted. "The Upper Thirds can put *Don't get a gripey tummy* on their stupid belts." She said it quite loud enough for the gang of Upper Thirds sitting on the other side of the room to hear, but there was only a frozen silence in response.

"Miss Evie!" Sarah came bustling up the stairs towards the nursery, and Max ran yapping to greet her, scrabbling at her skirt with his tiny paws. "Get off me, you daft dog. Miss Evie, the butcher's boy's just been, and he says there's a ship wrecked over at Saltwick Nab."

"On the rocks?" Evie jumped up, and Kitty's crochet slid off her lap unnoticed as she stared at Sarah.

"Yes, miss. Happened early this morning, so Joe Barker told me. There's people all over the town going out there with blankets, and flasks of tea for the rescuers." She wound her fingers in her apron. "My oldest brother's in the lifeboat crew, Miss Evie."

Evie nodded. Sarah had four brothers, all of them fishermen. "Joe said that they tried to launch it this morning, but the sea was too rough. They had to lift the smaller boat, the *John Fielden*, over the pier wall – eight foot tall, that wall is! And then they dragged it along the scar to go out from the beach instead."

Evie nodded. "Is it – is it a big ship that's on the rocks?" she asked anxiously, wondering how many people would be aboard.

"A big steamer, by what Joe said, miss, with some outlandish name. But she's a hospital ship, on her way to France and packed full of nurses and doctors, poor things. She's only a few hundred yards offshore, but the sea's so rough they can't get to her. The lifeboat took a few people off, the four nurses and some of the doctors, but that's only a few of them."

"Is Mama in?" Evie asked, glancing towards the door. "We should ask her if we should go and take blankets, like you said."

"Cook has some soup we could send, miss. But Mrs Maitland is resting, and you know she doesn't like to be disturbed. I don't like to take blankets without asking."

Evie sighed faintly, guiltily. School had almost made her forget about Alecky, and Kitty was the same. The trains were still set out on the floor – she'd had to step over them to go and talk to Sarah – but they were thick with dust. Every so often, something would remind her, and it was as if a hand had squeezed around her heart, but most of the time she was too busy to remember.

Even the war, growing closer day by day, hadn't dulled the edges of Mama's memory. She spent most of her time sitting in her room, looking at a photograph of Alecky that stood on a little table, with a posy of flowers next to it. Occasionally she would brighten up – as she had been diverted for a day or two when teaching Kitty to crochet – but then she sank back into a deep sadness.

"No. . ." she murmured. "We'd better not bother her. But I'm sure she would say we ought to help, Sarah. Don't you think?" Evie nibbled the inside of her lip and looked at Sarah worriedly. It was silly that Sarah had to ask her – she was sure that the maid knew far better than she did what they ought to be doing.

"Can we go?" Kitty asked hopefully. "I can carry blankets, or the soup." Her eyes were shining excitedly. "We should hurry up, Evie, or everyone'll be rescued before we get there."

"They won't, Miss Kitty—" Sarah started to say, and then she broke off, glancing at Evie. "She's been on those rocks a good few hours, it's nearly ten now, miss. Joe said she's already broken in half."

"Kitty, maybe you shouldn't go." Evie caught her little sister's hand. "Those rocks are so dangerous, you know they are. That's why there's always been a buoy there to warn the ships. But they took the bell and the light off it, because of the war."

Kitty swallowed. "If there's going to be people drowned, it's even more reason we should help." She looked up, the pinkness of her cheeks fading,

66

and Evie knew she was thinking of Alecky, lying in bed in a white nightgown instead of the striped pyjamas he loved, with his hands folded over each other on top of the sheet. "I won't be scared," Kitty whispered.

"Will you come too, Sarah?" Evie asked. "Is Cook heating the soup up? The blankets are on the top shelf of the linen cupboard, I think. There must be some that are old, ones that Mama wouldn't mind us giving away."

They hurried down the stairs, with the dogs bounding around them, slowing to a creep when they reached the floor below where Mama was.

Mrs Dixon was already pouring soup into a metal can with a lid, while the scullery maid was at the table packing a basket of white enamelled mugs to drink it from, and slices of bread wrapped in a napkin.

"Do you think this is war work, Evie?" Kitty asked, looking hopefully at the basket.

"I suppose so."

They set off, Kitty with the basket, and Evie with the soup can, and Sarah following after them with piles of blankets. Evie had shut Brandy and Max in the garden as they thought it was a picnic and expected to go too, and she was worried that they would bark and disturb Mama if they were indoors.

The town seemed to be oddly busy and empty at the same time. There was hardly anyone in and out of the shops, but little knots of people had gathered here and there, anxiously exchanging news. There were several other passers-by with baskets of food and flasks of coffee, and Evie noticed approving nods as they saw what the girls were carrying.

"The sea's so rough!" Evie gasped, as they came on to the flats below the East Cliff. The waves were pounding on to the rocks, the tide hissing and thundering. Kitty huddled against her, eyeing the water. Miss Jennings and Mama had always taken them to the sandy beach below the West Cliff, and this wilder, rockier landscape was fearsome.

They began to pick their way gingerly between the boulders, and Evie wondered if perhaps they should go back and climb the steps to the abbey so they could watch from the clifftop instead. But she couldn't see how they would be able to pass out the soup and blankets from up there – there was no path down to the beach. There were plenty of other watchers milling about on the scar, so it had to be safe.

Sarah shifted her bundle of blankets under one arm and took Kitty's hand. "Be careful, miss," she said to Evie. "You could break an ankle along here. Oh my God!"

"Sarah!" Kitty squeaked, in a sort of delighted horror, and then she whispered, "Oh!"

Evie stopped trying to see where she was putting her feet, and looked out, towards the sea. The ship was there, shrouded in the heavy spray. It seemed to loom up out of the waves, leaning horribly sideways, and Evie could just pick out tiny figures gathered together against the railings.

"It's so close!" She clutched at Sarah's arm. "Why can't they get those people off? Surely they can reach them?"

"They've tried, miss," a man passing by broke in. "T'lifeboat took off another eighteen men just now, but it's too damaged – holed in two places, from dragging it across t'scar here, and t'rough sea's just made it worse."

"Didst tha see my brother?" Sarah asked him anxiously. "Richard Eglon, he's t'coxswain, is he safe?" Her Yorkshire accent thickened as she spoke to the fisherman, Evie noticed. She much watch her words so carefully, up at the house.

"All t'crew are safe, don't you worry. You can't go along there wi' t'young ladies, tide's rising, t'isn't safe. Everyone's coming back. They've abandoned t'lifeboat on the beach now – tide's too high to launch her again, even if she weren't holed. It's getting near t'foot of t'cliffs."

Evie looked at him properly, and realized that he was soaked almost to his shoulders, his thick woollen jumper dark with water. "Oh! Were you on the lifeboat?"

The man shook his head. "Nay, miss. Helping ter launch it."

"Would you like some soup? You must be so cold." Evie held up the can to show him, and he nodded eagerly, and accepted a mug from Kitty's basket and held it out for Evie to fill. "Will tha take this up t'cliffs, miss? There's some thought of bringing another lifeboat along from Upgang. No one wants ter leave them poor souls. Some of us have been dahn here since t'maroons were fired early this morning."

"Of course we will." Evie nodded. She was shamefully relieved that they were not to carry on along the scar. If even the fishermen who'd been helping to launch the lifeboat thought it wasn't safe, it wasn't cowardly to turn back.

"Must we go up the steps?" Kitty whispered.

"Don't be such a lazy object!" Evie hissed back. "Think of those poor men out on the ship!"

"I wasn't being lazy! I only meant, isn't there another path?" Kitty sighed.

"You know quite well there isn't. It won't take long."

"It will," Kitty muttered. "How can a hundred and ninety-nine steps not take long? Don't be absurd."

Lugging the heavy can of soup up the Church Stairs, Evie rather regretted having been so stern. She could hardly stop and pant when she'd told Kitty the climb was nothing. It was only when they reached the top that she remembered they hadn't been to St Mary's since the funeral. They would have to pass Alecky's grave as they cut through the churchyard and past the ruined abbey to the cliffs. Alecky's headstone hadn't yet been placed, but they knew where the grave was.

"He would have been so excited to see a shipwreck," Evie whispered, as they looked at the patch of broken ground, the turf still dryish and yellowing.

72

"He wouldn't have done," Kitty pointed out. "Miss Jennings would never have let us come."

Sarah, who was standing behind them, murmured, "Perhaps I'd better take tha back. It in't t'place for young ladies."

"It is!" Evie whirled round. "Or it should be! One of my friends at school has a sister who's gone to London to look after refugees, and David wants to fight in the war, and Frank Armstrong from Daddy's offices has already joined up and he's only just left school. We have to do *something*, and we're only bringing soup, Sarah, it isn't even a little bit dangerous – we're only going to stand on the clifftop now, we're not even down on the scar."

"Miss Kitty's right, though." Sarah hefted the blankets up again, her face shiny with steps and guilt. "Miss Jennings never would have let tha."

"I expect Miss Jennings is doing war work, actually," Kitty suggested. "She was always ever so keen on us doing our duty, especially if we whispered during the sermon in church. She used to go on about it for ages. I expect she'd be *proud* of us, Sarah."

"Umm," Sarah murmured. "Oh, get on then." And she sighed, and bobbed her head towards the grave, as if she didn't know what else to do.

The view from the clifftop was almost more frightening than the closer view from the scar. Looking down, it was even clearer what a terrifying state the ship was in. Something that huge was wrong, so close in to the shore. It dwarfed the abandoned lifeboat, which was splintering against the rocks already. There was a great crowd of people watching from the cliffs, but there was no chatter, only worried whispering. Everyone in Whitby knew someone who worked a fishing boat, or had some connection with the sea. This wasn't just a show, not for them.

"What are they going to do?" Evie whispered, drawing closer to Sarah. The maid's face was awful, the skin draining pale under her hot cheeks.

That was her brother's lifeboat breaking apart down there.

"I don't know, miss, I don't know. What can they do? Look at t'sea! They can't take t'other lifeboat out of t'harbour, they said, it's too wild. And I don't see how they can bring t' Upgang boat – what are they going ter do with it when it gets here? It's no good up on top of t'cliff. Oh my God, just look at those poor souls. . ."

The sea was rising again, the waves growing even fiercer. The ship had been broken into pieces when it first ran aground on the rocks, and now the different parts were separating and sinking. Most of the tiny dark figures were on the main central part of the deck, but there were men clinging to the stern too – surely fewer of them now than when she and Kitty and Sarah had been down on the scar? Had they jumped?

"The wave!" Kitty gasped. "It's going over them, Evie!"

A deep groan ran through the crowd as a huge

wave swelled and rose behind the ship, building in a great heavy bulge and sweeping over the stern.

When it passed, the back half of the ship had gone – turned right over and disappeared – and the clinging figures had gone with it. Someone sobbed loudly, and Evie felt Sarah's arms go around her and Kitty. "Should never have brought tha," the maid whispered faintly. "Never."

"What's happened to them?" Kitty asked, her voice muffled by Sarah's coat. "They can't just have gone. . ."

"It swept them away," Evie told her numbly. "But . . . perhaps they had life jackets on. They'll be brought in on the tide." Miserably, the three of them gazed at the black rocks and the water boiling and churning around them. That was where the men would end up. It seemed impossible that anyone could survive.

There was a scuffling and a fussing from further along the cliff, and Evie heard someone say, "Stand back and give her some air."

"Someone's fainted," Kitty reported, leaning out in front of Sarah, until the maid hissed and pulled her back from the edge. "Maybe we should give her one of our blankets?"

"Do you have blankets to spare, miss?" a young man passing along behind asked. "I'm part of the St John Ambulance Brigade, we'll take them."

Sarah thrust the blankets into his arms, and Kitty waved the basket of mugs at him. "We've got soup as well. Will you find any of those poor men?"

"One man came in close to the piers, swimming, but that was earlier this morning, when the tide wasn't so high." He stared out to sea, a grim expression on his face. "We'd be glad to take the soup for the rescuers, miss, as well. Here, Jack, can you carry these?" He beckoned to a boy about David's age who was coming along the path, wearing a red cross on an armband. "Take this down to the others. We can bring the mugs back to you, miss." He pulled out a notebook and offered it to Sarah, but she pushed it into Evie's hands. "We'll tuck your address in the basket."

Evie nodded and wrote down their address. The ambulance man tore out the page and put it under the napkin. Then he tipped his hat to Evie and Sarah and Kitty, and hurried on.

"I suppose we should go back," Evie murmured. "There isn't anything else we can do to help." But it was so hard to walk away – it felt as if they were abandoning the tiny figures on the ship's bridge. The crowd of watchers were all willing them to safety.

"We'd better," Sarah said. "It can't be far off midday now, your ma will miss us. I've got ter serve t'dinner."

"I would rather stay," said Evie. "I don't want to go back, and . . . and leave them." She turned back to look at the ship.

"You could tell Mama we're out with friends from school," Kitty suggested. "I think that's one of the boys from my class down there." She pointed further along the path. "So it's not *actually* a lie."

"What about thy dinner?" Sarah asked doubtfully.

Evie shivered. "I'm not hungry."

"I'm not either." Kitty shook her head. "I expect I will be soon, but I don't mind. I want to stay."

Sarah nodded. "I'll tell Mrs Maitland that tha's gone out. But tha come back soon, Miss Evie. Tha can't stay out once it's dark."

Evie gave her a quick, tight smile. They both knew that Mama probably wouldn't ask where they were, and Daddy, if he came back to the house for lunch, would be unlikely to notice that they were gone. Evie turned back into the biting wind off the sea, blinking away tears that weren't really to do with the cold.

Sarah headed away back down the path, and Evie slid her arm around Kitty's waist. Her little sister leaned on her, and they stared at the ship, wishing for the tiny dark figures to hold tight, to be brave, to wait...

Chapter Four

The next morning, Evie woke early and hurried on her clothes, pattering down the stairs to the kitchen. She arrived in the middle of the servants' breakfast, and the four of them stared at her in surprise. Mrs Dixon set down her cup of tea and glared.

"I'm sorry," Evie whispered. "I only wondered – is there any more news?" The day before, she and Kitty had left a while after the Upgang lifeboat had arrived, hauled over land to the top of the cliffs on a dray drawn by six great horses. The girls had watched the crew fussing around it, wondering what could possibly be done with it now. There was a path down to Saltwick Bay from further along the clifftop, but Evie wasn't sure even one horse could get down it, let alone a team pulling a boat. But then the lifeboat was lifted off, and teams of men crowded round with thick ropes. They lowered the boat down the cliff to the beach, two hundred and fifty feet below. Evie had clapped and even cheered with the crowd as the boat reached the rocks – but then nothing had happened. The tide was still too high, and the sea too rough. After all that work, the lifeboat sat useless on the beach, while the crowd on the top of the cliff yelled angrily down at the crew. She had covered Kitty's ears.

The ship was gradually breaking up, and it seemed that nothing could be done. She and Kitty had trailed home mid-afternoon, and Evie had gone to bed, cold as ice, and cried.

Mrs Dixon smiled at her, and nodded at the scullery maid. "Fetch Miss Evie a cup, Mary-Ann.

There's just about enough in t'pot. You look chilled to the bone, miss."

"Thank you." Evie accepted the cup, and sipped the strong tea gratefully. "It's almost low tide now, isn't it?" she asked Sarah. "Does that mean they'll try again?"

"Stretcher parties found eleven bodies on t'rocks at low tide last night," Sarah told her.

"Eleven! But – but how many are left, then?"

Sarah sighed. "I went down my ma's this morning ter ask. A good many, and they're still alive, and signalling t'shore. 'A long way to Tipperary', they sent this morning! But the sea's still too rough for the Upgang boat to reach them, and t'rockets are doing no good at all." She sniffed, and gulped her tea. "T'motor lifeboat was coming from Redcar, miss, but it's broken down."

"I was sure, by now..."

"You can take some more soup, Miss Evie. A boy brought the can and the mugs back last night." Mrs Dixon stood up briskly. "A vegetable broth. I'll have it ready after breakfast. If tide's low again now, there might be more poor souls trying to swim. They'll need something hot, and you'll be able to get along t'scar and take it to them." She hesitated. "You'd better mention it to your father."

Evie nodded. They could explain yesterday away – Daddy out at the office, not wanting to disturb Mama. Going out to the cliffs again today, after sitting silent through breakfast, could not be anything but deceit.

She went back upstairs after she had finished the tea, to prime Kitty. They were quiet all through breakfast, though Evie did try to peer at the newspaper, to see if there was anything about the ship. It was too early for it to be reported though, perhaps.

"Daddy," she murmured as he folded up the paper and laid his napkin beside his plate. "May Kitty and I go along the beach under the East Cliff today? Mrs Dixon has some soup we could take to give to the men working on the beach. We – we took some up to the clifftop yesterday, you see, and the St John's Ambulance men were very grateful."

"They brought the soup can back," Kitty added reassuringly. "And today we can tie a label on it with the address."

Evie glanced quickly between her mother and father. Mama looked surprised – almost normally so. "A soup can?"

"For the men trying to rescue the shipwrecked sailors, Mama. The sailors too, if any are washed in."

"I told you about it last night, Helen," their father said gently. "The ship caught on the rocks at Saltwick, do you remember?"

"Oh! Oh, yes, of course I do." She gave herself a little shake, Evie saw, and seemed to wake up. "You went up there on your own?"

"No, Mama, Sarah came with us. We would have asked you, but you were resting. Sarah's brother is in the lifeboat crew, you see. She was worried about him."

"Oh..." Mama glanced at the window, and then back at Evie, looking lost. She blinked and sat up straighter, trying to claw back some sort of motherly worry. "You must be very careful. The tides, you know."

Evie nodded. "We will." She got up and put her arm very gently around her mother's shoulders, as if she might break. Mama felt cold under her lace-collared blouse, and Evie wanted to cling to her tighter, but she didn't. "I promise."

"Are we going along the beach this time?" Kitty asked as they went down the front steps.

"I think so. The tide's low for another hour or two. I expect quite a lot of people will be doing the same. It's safe enough. Oh, no..." Evie turned at the eager scrabbling behind them, and the two dogs flung themselves at her legs, whining affectionately. Sarah was hurrying after them, looking flustered. "I'm sorry, miss. They got out t'side door after you – Mary-Ann opened it without thinking. Come here, come on." She tried to flap her apron at Brandy and Max, who ignored her completely.

"No, Brandy, no, Max. I'm sorry." Evie set down the soup can and caught Brandy's collar. "Kitty, grab Max! I promise we'll come back soon and walk you. Yes. Yes we will." Max let out a miserable wail, and Brandy stared at her with eyes like melting toffee. "Oh, don't do that. . ." Evie murmured. "We can't take you, it would be dangerous. Especially not you," she added to Max. He was only little, and not very well trained at walking to heel. When they took both dogs out, Brandy would pace along with a noble expression, as though he was trying to make it clear that Max was nothing to do with him. The little dachshund darted about, tripping Evie up and yapping at strange carriages, and always, always squatting in the most embarrassing places, so that Evie had to pretend not to know what he was doing.

After they had shut the dogs back in, the girls walked down through the town to the beach, and along the scar. Now that the tide was low, there was far more sand to walk on, and it felt safer. There were several others carrying flasks and blankets, some of them running along the beach.

"Perhaps there's been news?" Evie wondered, as two fishergirls hurried by with shawls pulled up over their heads. They walked on faster.

"There are people in the water!" Kitty gasped as they came closer to the wreck. "Look, Evie, I think they're pulling someone out."

Stretching from the beach into the sea was a long line of men, all holding hands. Those on the beach were clearly anchoring those further out, the line leading far into the sea. The furthest man was shoulder deep, eagerly reaching towards a dark shape in the water.

"That's wreckage," Evie murmured doubtfully. But it was so hard to tell, and then another wave tossed the odd lump over, and they could see it was a man, his hair sea-darkened and his face pale. Evie squeezed her fingers tight around the metal handle of the can, willing the line of men on. Then she cried out delightedly as the end man seized hold of the sailor's life jacket, and began to pass him slowly back towards the shore.

"Evie!" Someone was calling her across the beach. Evie looked around and waved shyly at Elaine, one of the prefects they had met on their first morning at school. She was trailed by a plump and elderly-looking black Labrador, who sniffed curiously at Kitty's basket.

"Hello! Oh, you've brought food." Elaine nodded approvingly.

"We came yesterday, and people seemed glad of it," Evie explained. "We gave it to someone from the ambulance brigade – soup and blankets."

"It's very important to keep the casualties warm," Elaine agreed. "I did a course in ambulance last term. I came to see if I could do anything to help, but I think you had the better idea – there are far more experienced people here than me. All I did was help to calm a poor woman having hysterics up on the clifftop – her husband was on board."

Kitty crouched down to stroke the Labrador's smooth head. "You see, Evie, we should have just brought Brandy and Max with us."

Elaine sighed. "I didn't actually want to bring her, but my mother doesn't like me going out alone. Quite what Mama thinks Jet is going to do to help, I don't know. At least she's had the sense not to go swimming today. She loves the water, but this is a bit much, even for her."

"Will that poor man be all right?" Evie asked, looking worriedly at the sailor, who was being helped stumbling out of the waves in the middle of a knot of rescuers, his arms around their necks.

"He's walking," Elaine said. "And conscious. I expect he's frozen, though. The lifeboats just can't get to the wreck, and several of the men have decided to swim for it." She shuddered. "I can't imagine it – deciding your best chance is to jump into . . . that." She gestured at the sea, so cold and grey.

"I know." Evie had spent so much time on the sandy beach below the West Cliff with Miss Jennings, building castles and looking for seashells and starfish in the little rock pools. They had still gone out on wet and windy days, of course, but in her memory the sea was blue, or at least bluish. It didn't have this sullen, angry, hungry look.

"Shall we walk further up, and I can see if I recognize anyone you could give the soup to?" Elaine suggested, and Evie nodded eagerly. Half a term at school was quite long enough for them to know that Elaine was royalty, compared to two small girls at the lower end of the school.

"The St John's Ambulance Brigade have set up an emergency hospital," Elaine explained. "One of the summer teahouses, Miss Agar's. It's very rough – there isn't even a tap, but luckily they could gather the rainwater. I expect bread and soup will be very welcome there. Oh, look." She hurried over to a man in a dark coat, with another of the red cross armbands, and started to talk to him, pointing out Evie and Kitty. He smiled wearily at the girls, and took the basket and the soup can when they held them out. "I would go back home now," he suggested to all of them. "The storm's worsening again. I don't know how much longer the ship will hold together."

Evie wanted to say that she wasn't scared, but she couldn't. It had been so horrifying, the stern of the ship turning over and disappearing the day before. She couldn't bear to see the rest break up, with no rescue happening.

"The lifeboats?" she asked hopefully.

"Too rough for any of the rowing boats," the man explained. "Whitby needs a motor lifeboat of our own. If any good could come of this disaster, surely it's that."

"They've sent for another motor lifeboat, haven't they?" Elaine asked. "But I suppose with the gale it takes ages even for a motorboat to come down the coast."

"Are we going home?" Kitty whispered in Evie's ear. The man who had been pulled out of the sea by the lifeline was balanced on a stretcher now, ready to be carried up the cliff path. The wind was rising again, and Kitty was clutching at her hat and looking enviously at the fishergirls, who wore shawls drawn up over their heads like cloaks, and weren't troubled with hatpins.

Evie nodded. "Unless we go up on the cliff again – but it feels—" She stopped, unable to explain. Part of her wanted to be there again, holding her thumbs for the poor sailors to wish them luck, but it was all going so dreadfully wrong. They should be cheering on the gallant lifeboat crews, not watching the last survivors weigh up their chances against the waves. It was – she felt – as if they would be treating the shipwreck as one of those adventure stories David had left in the nursery bookcase, filled with Disaster and Heroism and Plucky British Lads. She didn't want to hear about sailors heroically sacrificing themselves for their fellow men just now, she only wanted them all to be safe – and it was becoming clearer and clearer that they wouldn't be.

"Are you going to stay?" Evie asked Elaine shyly, and the older girl sighed. "No. May Jet and I walk back through the town with you? Somehow I don't want to be on my own."

Evie nodded, and envied Kitty for being young enough to slip her hand into Elaine's as they turned to walk back along the scar. Kitty could prattle on about Brandy, and how well trained Jet was, without any self-consciousness at all. How could she chatter about school now? But at least it meant Evie could be quiet, and let her little sister's gossip wash over her.

Kitty raced off ahead, leaving Evie and Elaine together, as they came to St Hilda's Terrace. The older girl lived further along towards the West Cliff, she'd told them.

"I'm sorry – she goes on so," Evie murmured.

"She stopped me thinking about the ship." Elaine smiled at her. "I'm grateful, Evie, I promise. You look worn out, you know. Did you have nightmares? You were there yesterday too, weren't you?"

"I hate it that no one can do anything," Evie explained. "I know they're *trying* – firing all those rockets to send ropes, and sending for the lifeboats from all over the place. But it's worse somehow when the ship is so close. I keep imagining how it must feel, to be able to see the land and not reach it."

"Yes." Elaine sighed, and they walked on silently, Evie shivering a little in the rain. They weren't far from their house when she saw Kitty dashing back towards them, with Brandy and Max on leads. Jet peered forward, and started to beat her tail slowly.

"I thought you'd like to meet them," Kitty panted. "Aren't they gorgeous?"

"Max will get cold," Evie murmured. "He's so little that the puddles go halfway up him."

Brandy and Jet were sniffing at each other in a slow, dignified sort of way, while Max yapped excitedly around their feet.

"Brandy is an Airedale," Kitty said proudly. "He's Daddy's, really, but he loves me and Evie more. And Max was Evie's for her birthday. He's very badly behaved."

"He's only a baby." Evie scooped him up, and held him as he wriggled wildly in her arms, whining with delight and trying to lick her ears.

"He's a darling." Elaine reached in to stroke him, and then added, "But I suppose..." Then she trailed off. "I suppose dachshunds are quite hard to train," she went on, rather quickly.

Evie nodded, wondering what she had actually been going to say.

"Sarah said that Mama had been asking if we were back, Evie," Kitty remembered suddenly. "She said not to be long. Would you like to come and visit?" she added to Elaine, and the older girl smiled at her while Evie made horrified faces behind her back. They couldn't take Elaine up to the nursery, they just couldn't, and where else was there?

"Another day I would, but I'm all wet and windblown. I'll see you back at school, I expect." She looked back across the town – they could see the abbey ruins up on the cliff quite clearly. The wreck wasn't far beyond. "We'll hope for good news," she sighed. Evie nodded, and buried her nose in Max's plush fur. She didn't think Elaine sounded very hopeful.

"Wake up, miss! Miss Evie! They've done it!"

Evie turned over and blinked up at Sarah. It was only just getting light. "What is it?" she murmured. "Are we late for school?"

"No, miss, no. It's t'ship – t'motor lifeboat from Tynemouth, it's bringing t'men off t'wreck."

"Truly? Oh!" Evie flung her arms around Sarah's neck and hugged her. Then she scrambled out of bed to find her clothes. "Now? It's happening now? Oh, I have to wake Kitty."

"They'll bring them back in to harbour, miss. Half the town will be down there, I should think. Cook did say perhaps she could send some tea. . ."

"I'm getting dressed," Evie said, pulling on her stockings and hopping along the passage to Kitty's room. "We'll be down in a moment, Sarah, don't go without us!"

The gale was still blowing as they hurried down the hill towards the harbour. "Where will she come in?" Evie panted, and Sarah shook her head uncertainly. "One of t'jetties by t'bridge? Look, there's a crowd there already." They ran out on to the bridge and joined the knots of people gazing down the river towards the open sea.

"Is there any news?" Sarah gasped out to a woman standing near.

"It was t'boat from Tynemouth," the woman told her eagerly. "Came in overnight, and they loaded her up with oil, ter pour on t'water."

"What for?" Kitty whispered loudly, and the woman smiled at her.

"It calms the water, flower. Still terrible rough out there, seethee?" Then she clutched at Sarah's arm and shrieked. "Look! There they be!"

Evie and Kitty leaned over the iron rail of the bridge, peering through the rain. The low purring sound of the engine came over the wind, and as the heavily laden lifeboat drew up to a quay close to the bridge, church bells began to ring all through Whitby.

The boat was crammed with men, all so pale and exhausted that they hardly seemed to hear the cheering. They were half lifted out of the boat, and a slow procession of stumbling figures began to climb the steps. Kitty poked Evie in the side. "Look, he's wearing pyjamas," she whispered. "And almost none of them have got shoes on."

"The ship hit the rocks when most of them were in bed," Evie pointed out. "They must just have run out in what they were wearing." She pulled her coat tighter around her.

"They do look badly," Sarah murmured. "All cut about."

Evie nodded. "I wish we'd brought more blankets. Shall we pass that flask along, do you think? We can't get any closer."

They watched eagerly as the survivors were wrapped up in blankets and handed mugs of tea, and then Evie leaned so far over the bridge that Sarah snatched at her coat, and yelped, "Have a care, miss!"

"Yes, but Sarah, look!" Evie turned back to her, laughing. "That man there in the dark overcoat, he's carrying a cat!"

Sarah frowned doubtfully across the water, and then nodded. "Happen you're right, Miss Evie. A little black cat, is it?"

"That's t'captain," the woman next to them said. "He do look grand."

"He's got it tucked in his coat. He saved the

ship's cat!" Evie stopped laughing suddenly. More than two whole days on the wrecked ship, with waves washing over them, and all those failed attempts at rescue, but they'd still made sure to save their cat.

"Don't cry, Evie!" Kitty stared at her. "Why're you crying now, when they're saved, silly?"

Chapter Five

The captain of the hospital ship *Rohilla* had been awarded a medal by the RSPCA, Daddy told them at breakfast a few weeks later. "Though I shouldn't think he's too happy about it," he added. "He and the crew are convinced that they hit a mine, but apparently the inquest weren't too sure. The ship was seven miles off her course, and the coastguard was signalling to her that she was about to hit the rocks, but they didn't see." He sighed, and shook the paper. "Still . . . eighty-three lives lost seems nothing, when you read the news from Ypres. Casualties in the thousands."

"Thousands?" Kitty said, in a small voice.

Her father looked at her, and seemed to realize that he was talking in front of an eight-year-old.

"The Germans too," he murmured, and glanced towards his wife. Then he turned the paper round, holding it out to Evie and Kitty. "Have you girls seen this? Perhaps it would be something for you and your friends at school. A change from the endless knitting."

Evie stared at him in surprise. She'd had no idea he knew about the committee, or that he'd even noticed them knitting.

"Every time I see you, there's a trail of wool." He smiled. "It's a very good idea. Look, up here at the top of the page."

"The Soldiers' and Sailors' Christmas Gift Fund," Evie read out. "Oh, Princess Mary!" she added admiringly. She and Kitty had seen photographs of the princess, who was only seventeen. She was very beautiful, in a grand, remote sort of way.

"What is it?" Kitty demanded, getting up to read over her shoulder.

"A fund for a Christmas present 'for every sailor afloat and every soldier at the front'. She says, *Will you help me?* Oh, we must! Daddy, can I tear out just that little bit of the paper, to show Sybil and Grace and Dot? Have you read the other side?"

"I can sacrifice it," he murmured, tearing out the corner of the page. "What will you girls do to raise money, though?"

Evie had been thinking of sending her pocket money, but she had spent it all on wool. "Would Mrs Dixon let us make toffee?" she wondered. "We could put it in pretty paper and sell it at school."

"Mmm. You'll have to ask her. She came to me the other day quite worried about the grocer's order, since the prices have risen so much." But he drew a handful of change out of his trouser pocket, and passed a shilling to Evie. "I expect she will, if you tell her why. There. For the sugar and such."

*

Grace, it turned out, had a very lavishly equipped nursery with its own kitchen for making nursery tea. Since she was so much younger than her brother, the nursery was left all to her now, and it made a perfect sweet factory. Mrs Dixon supplied a recipe for toffee, and also suggested (once she'd discovered that none of the sweet-making would be happening in her pristine kitchen) peppermint sugar mice, coloured pink with cochineal, and given little string tails. The mice were pretty, and unlike the toffee they used no butter, which Mrs Dixon said was getting dearer than hen's teeth due to the food shortages. They were extremely popular, especially with Kitty's Prep class, priced at a penny each. This was quite expensive compared to a sweet shop, but Evie and the others had the advantage of being there at morning break, with baskets full.

Miss Douthett had been a little doubtful when they first set up shop, but Evie showed her the newspaper cutting, and the OXO tin Mrs Dixon had given her to collect the money. Then Sybil, who was good at arithmetic, explained very carefully how the first shilling had been laid out on ingredients, and how they meant to plough back one penny out of every three to keep them in peppermint oil, and paper bags, and sugar. After that Miss Douthett had nodded feebly, and said she would mention it to Miss Davidson, and it was a very good idea, very patriotic. She even let them use the art room at dinner time, to paint price cards. Evie painted a portrait of Princess Mary, surrounded by two crossed flags, to put in the basket behind the sweets. The princess's nose was rather too large, but Evie balanced it out with a really impressive crown and no one complained.

Christmas seemed to come much faster than usual, since they were so busy. School was to finish a few days before Christmas, with the grand Christmas concert in the hall. Neither Evie nor Kitty were part of the concert – it was mostly the older pupils – but a week beforehand, Miss

Davidson swept into the Third Form classroom and stood by Miss Douthett's desk, looking over the top of her pince-nez spectacles. Everyone stood up hurriedly – the headmistress hardly ever came to the form rooms, and the Thirds usually only saw her at morning prayers.

"Evie Maitland. Where is Evie?"

"Here," Evie said, her voice coming out in a squeak of panic. Someone giggled, and Miss Davidson swept a quelling glance around the room.

"My dear, Miss Douthett tells me that you were responsible for the craze for pink sugar mice currently sweeping the school."

"I – um – yes, Miss Davidson," Evie agreed, wondering if there was a school rule against sugar mice. But surely Miss Davidson wouldn't have called her "dear" if she were about to be expelled?

"And you are selling them to raise money for Princess Mary's Christmas Fund?"

"Yes, Miss Davidson."

"How much have you raised so far?"

Evie couldn't resist beaming at her. "Sixteen shillings!" It seemed a huge amount of money. "But it's all of our form, Miss Davidson. The Lower Thirds have a War Aid Committee, and all of us made something."

"Extremely enterprising, girls." Miss Davidson nodded approvingly. "Your patriotic feeling is highly commended. I would like to suggest that you have a little stall at the Christmas concert."

There was a clear gasp around the form room at this. The Christmas concert was special, everyone knew that. Only the very best performances were allowed, and the folk dancers and the drama society had been fighting over the assembly hall for weeks. Selling their sweets at the concert was like the official seal of approval.

"Thank you, Miss Davidson," Evie whispered, flashing excited, awed looks at the rest of her form – and pointedly ignoring the Upper Thirds, who seemed to have gone a bit green.

*

"We'll be late!" Kitty hissed.

"No, we won't," Evie retorted automatically. But she didn't need Kitty peeking into her satchel to know that she was probably right.

"Ooohhh! It's a quarter to nine, Evie, we're going to be sooo late!" Kitty wailed. "What's Grace doing?"

"I'm here! I slipped over on the top stairs with the basket of toffee." Grace thrust a basket at Evie and hurried down her front steps. "Are we dreadfully late?"

"Did you spill this all down the stairs?" Evie looked at the striped paper packets suspiciously. "Is there carpet fluff on this toffee, Grace? We're selling it at the Christmas concert, it has to be perfect!"

"It was only the packets," Grace assured her. "And toffee can't really break, or at any rate it doesn't matter if it does. It would have been much worse if I'd flung the mice down the stairs. We'd better run. Don't panic, Kitty, Evie is Miss

Davidson's favourite pupil just now, and besides, everyone's so up in the air about the concert, they probably won't even notice that we're late. Miss Douthett was so worried about all the decorated programmes yesterday that it took her until dinner time to notice that Dot hadn't come to school because of her bad tooth."

They scurried through the streets to the school, lugging the baskets of sweets for their stall. They had decided to bring everything before school, so that they could arrange it in the dinner hour, rather than later on in their best dresses, but their timing was decidedly off. Evie just hoped Grace was right, and everyone was too distracted to care.

It was past nine by the time they were dashing across the playing fields – everyone would be going into assembly. Perhaps they could sneak in at the back, Evie thought, or maybe lurk outside in the corridor and mingle with everyone coming out?

"Goodness, you three are late," someone

called, and Evie's shoulders slumped. No chance of sneaking in then. Then she realized it was Elaine, huddled in a scarf against the wind, and brightened a little. Would she help, if they explained?

"We've brought all the sweets for our stall," she said, holding up her huge basket. "It took ages to bring them all from Grace's house, you see—"

"What are you doing out here?" Kitty interrupted, and Elaine laughed at her.

"Inspecting the hockey pitch. Miss Speirs is worried that it's too frozen for the match against Pickering later. I'm almost hoping it is – we could do without a match and the concert on the same afternoon. I'd rather not folk dance black and blue, thank you – the team from Pickering are lethal!" Her face changed as she spoke, and she spun round, facing towards the town and the sea. "What is that noise?"

"Thunder?" Grace said doubtfully. "I didn't see any lightning."

"It doesn't sound quite like thunder anyway," Evie started to say, when she heard Kitty scream, and there was a massive rumbling crash that Evie seemed to feel all through her body. She stood for a second clutching the basket, owl-eyed and frozen in a cloud of dust and soil. Then Elaine grabbed her by the arm and pulled her sharply sideways. Evie fell against her, and they rolled on the frosted grass, sweets spilling everywhere.

"The mice! They'll get all dirty," Evie wailed – but her voice sounded strange and far away, she could hardly hear it.

"Was that a bomb?" Grace said, her voice only an echoing whisper in Evie's damaged ears.

Evie looked up at Elaine, and saw the older girl nod slowly. A bomb! They were under attack, then? Was it an invasion?

"Kitty, come here," Evie gasped, reaching out for her little sister. But Kitty was still standing, gazing down at a jagged lump of metal that was lying on the grass beside them – almost exactly where Evie had been a moment before. Shrapnel, sunk half into the hockey pitch – part of the exploded case from the shell that had been fired across the town.

It was surrounded by little pink sugar mice.

Chapter Six

The explosions went on, and the four girls huddled together, Kitty burrowing into Evie the way she did when there was a thunderstorm. Evie could feel her sobbing, even though she couldn't hear it.

Elaine stood up, pulling the others with her, and shouted close to their faces, "We have to get under cover!"

Evie and Grace nodded, looking around for the nearest shelter. Was it safe to make a dash for the school?

"I think it's stopping," Grace mouthed. Her eyes

were open so wide that Evie could see the whites all around them. Evie stood up a little and peered around. There seemed to be no more of those booming crashes, and she couldn't see any fires or smoke. Perhaps Grace was right. Her ears were still ringing, but she was starting to hear a little better. "Shall we go back to the school?" Evie said, patting Elaine's arm so she could mouth the words.

Elaine shook her head. "No. Look."

Spilling out of the school building were a crowd of children, coats and hats on anyhow, many of them clinging to each other. Older students were shepherding Kitty's Prep class – obviously everyone was being sent home.

Miss Speirs, the gym mistress, strode over to them, clutching Elaine by the arms. "You're not hurt? I sent you outside! Thank goodness." She looked terribly shaken, Evie thought, almost as though she might cry, which was impossible. Then Miss Speirs took hold of Kitty's shoulders, turning her this way and that like a doll.

"She isn't hurt," Evie tried to say, "only scared." But her voice still echoed weirdly in her ears, and she couldn't tell how loudly she was talking. She shook her head helplessly.

"Concussion – the sound of the shells has half-deafened them," Miss Speirs said to Miss Davidson, who'd come hurrying up. "They were out here, all four."

"You must hurry home, girls," Miss Davidson told them. "The concert is cancelled. The school will reopen after the holidays." She looked at them worriedly. "Perhaps I should send a mistress with you."

"I can take them all, Miss Davidson," Elaine put in. "We don't live far apart." She pushed Kitty gently in front of her, leading them back across the field they'd crossed only a few minutes before.

They stumbled down the hill, stopping only once to gawk at a house halfway down that had no front wall any more. The pretty parlour stood open to the street, its wall a crumbled pile of bricks. The furniture seemed almost intact, only dusty.

"Was that what hit us?" Evie whispered, clutching at Grace's hand. Her ears were clearing a little now, she realized. Her hearing was coming back. "The same one?"

"Maybe a bit of it hit us," Elaine said slowly. "Or perhaps it was another shot altogether. I – I shouldn't think we'll ever know."

"Where are the people?" Kitty asked. "I've seen the lady who lived there. And her dog. She has a poodle, a little black one. He sits on the back of that sofa and watches out of the window. The one who always barks at us walking to school, Evie. He barked at us on our way up the hill, just now!"

"I expect he heard the shell coming," Evie said firmly. She wasn't sure if she believed what she was saying, but Kitty had to. "Brandy and Max would, wouldn't they? They know if the postman's opening the front gate, so of course they'd hear a shell coming. I should think this dog did too."

116

Then she looked round at the other three, her eyes darkening in panic. "Oh. . . Brandy and Max! Mama! Sarah and Mrs Dixon and Mary-Ann and Lizzie. . ." There had been so many of those deafening crashes – who knew where else they had fallen? She seized Kitty's hand and began to run, not even hearing Elaine call her back. She dragged Kitty after her, racing across the road and up the steep slope through the bare orchard and the market gardens, slipping in the winter mud. Elaine and Grace were following them, she noticed vaguely, as the climb slowed her and Kitty down. She couldn't stop seeing that house, so strangely open and fragile. How would Mama's room look, broken open like that?

"Mama. . ." Kitty was panting. "I want Mama. . ."

"I know. We're nearly there," Evie told her, tightening her grip on Kitty's hand as she hauled her out through the gates and on to St Hilda's Terrace. She scanned the road frantically, looking for fallen walls, or a haze of brick dust. Smoke, or even flames. But the road was still, and eerily quiet. Evie felt her breath ease a little. No strange, dolls' house, torn-open rooms.

She turned back to wave at Elaine and Grace, and then she and Kitty dashed through their front garden, the gate clanging behind them. She pulled the bell, and then hammered on the door with both her fists. There was wild barking behind it, and then it swung open, and Sarah hugged her and then Kitty, muttering prayers and wishes and furious panic into their hair. "They're here, Mrs Maitland," she shouted, over Max and Brandy's barking, and Evie looked up in surprise to see her mother running down the stairs. It was the first time in months they'd seen her move fast.

"I heard the bell. Oh, come here." Mama seized them, patting at their coats, holding their faces, even pulling off Kitty's felt school hat to inspect her hair. "You're safe. Both of you?"

"What about Daddy?" Evie begged, crouching

down to put her arms round Brandy. She could feel him trembling against her – the noise of the shells must have been terrifying for the dogs. Max crept over, belly to the carpet, and leaned on her legs. She reached down to rub his dense fur, over and over, until he sagged a little, and her own anxious breathing slowed.

"He telephoned," her mother said, letting out a shaking breath. "That dreadful jangling bell, I've hated it ever since he had it put in, but now... He's quite safe, although one of those awful shells landed in the street close to his office."

"A bit of one fell on Evie," Kitty put in, and their mother pressed her hand against her mouth. Her skin went grey – it was quite fascinating to watch.

"It didn't. Be quiet, Kitty," Evie hissed. "It was only close, Mama, I promise. It fell next to us on the school field."

"That school – I never wanted—" Their mother sat down on the last step of the stairs, as if her legs had given way. She pulled Kitty on to her lap, and

Max leaped up next to them and licked her cheek. She didn't even notice.

"Girls, you must run upstairs now, and pack," she murmured.

"Pack?" Evie frowned. "Where are we going?"

Her mother stared at her. "Inland, of course! It's an invasion, Evie. The Germans are coming, they could be here any moment. We have to get as far away as we possibly can. Perhaps we could go to the Stanforths', their house is so remote, out on the moor and not even close to the railway line..."

"The Germans are coming here?" Kitty echoed, winding her arms around her mother's neck.

"Yes, darling. So be a good girl and run upstairs to pack. I have to find the papers for the house, your father's will. Do you think the silver, Sarah? What should we take? I don't know – my poor lovely house, left abandoned for those cursed Huns."

"Mrs Dixon says she's staying, ma'am," Sarah put in. "She says her ankles won't stand it, running away."

"But she can't!" Mrs Maitland shook her head frantically. "Hasn't she read the papers? What about those poor Belgians? The most dreadful atrocities, innocents murdered by the German soldiers. She can't stay here!"

Sarah shook her head. "I know, ma'am, but I don't think she can see t'Hun coming in her kitchen, ma'am. She feels safer there."

"Ohhh," Mrs Maitland moaned, and then she pushed Kitty gently off her lap. "Upstairs, girls. Pack. Hurry. I'll go and talk to her."

Evie and Kitty retreated up the stairs as their mother and Sarah hurried to the kitchen.

"The Germans are coming!" Kitty said anxiously as Evie grabbed a little suitcase from the top of her wardrobe for her. "What should we do? I don't know what we're supposed to pack. Is it the same as for going to stay with Granny in London? Miss Jennings packed for me then, Evie!" Her voice was rising into a wail, and Brandy whined.

"Sshhh, it's all right. It'll be all right," Evie whispered, putting the suitcase down on Kitty's bed. She didn't know what to take either. Her best paintbox? Her sketchbook? Her seed pearl necklace? What were the things that she couldn't bear to lose? "No one said there was going to be an invasion, did they? Daddy was reading the newspaper at breakfast. Wouldn't they have said? Maybe it's all a mistake," she added doubtfully.

"France is awfully close," Kitty murmured. "Just across the sea. It would be so easy, and there's hardly any soldiers here at all. They've all gone to France and now the Germans have sneaked round behind them to invade us!"

"They couldn't." But Evie shivered, remembering the crashing of those exploding shells. The war was so much closer now. She could almost see the men in grey uniforms and coal scuttle helmets marching up through the town, and surrounding the house. "I don't know what to pack, Kitty. A nightdress and your toothbrush, I suppose."

"I'm taking my clock," Kitty said, suddenly stubborn.

"Yes, all right, if you *want* to have it stolen by a German soldier," Evie said nastily, and then regretted it as Kitty sank down on to her bed and started to cry. "Oh, I didn't mean it. I only – I'm scared, Kitty. I was being horrid because I'm scared."

"If I leave it *here* it'll be stolen," Kitty sobbed, clutching at Evie's coat. "And if I take it with me and they catch up with us it will be too."

Brandy leaped up on to the bed and tried to squirm his way into Evie's arms, leaving Max whining miserably on the floor.

"We *will* take the dogs, won't we?" Kitty asked, reaching out to rub the crinkly fur on Brandy's neck, and Evie stared at her.

"Of course we will!"

Kitty nodded. "I wasn't sure." Then she glanced up. "Listen. Was that the front door banging?"

"It must have been, look at the dogs."

Brandy leaped off the bed, and right over Max, racing for the stairs. The dachshund scuttled after him, furious at being left behind.

"Germans?" Kitty faltered.

Evie listened for a moment, clenching her fingers in Kitty's bedspread, and then let out a deep sigh. "No. It's Daddy. I can hear his voice. He'll know what we ought to take with us, Kitty." She took her little sister's hand, but Kitty pulled back and snatched up her clock, stuffing it into the deep pocket of her coat. Evie folded her lips together firmly and said nothing, and they ran back down the stairs. Their father was in the hallway, his arms around their mother.

"There you are! Evie, were you hurt?"

"I couldn't hear anything for a while. Everything's a bit muffled still, but that's all. Are we leaving?" She glanced worriedly down at Kitty. "We started to pack, but we don't know what to take. Miss Jennings always packed for us. And – if there is an invasion, what will happen to David?

He's on his way home from school, what if he's trapped and we can't find him?"

Her father smiled tiredly. "There is no invasion. I spoke to the chief constable. It was a naval attack only – two ships of the German fleet who slipped by our defences. Nothing more."

"Nothing more. . ." Mama said faintly. "It was enough, Charles! The town was under siege! How many people have been killed?"

Daddy shook his head. "I don't know. One of the coastguard, for certain, but there haven't been many other reports of casualties. Though we weren't the only town attacked." Evie saw him tighten his hands around Mama's arms, as if he thought he might need to hold her up. "There were more ships – one group hit Hartlepool earlier this morning, and the two that shelled us had already attacked Scarborough. There were a great many people killed in both towns," he added softly.

"Scarborough," Mama murmured, and her

eyes went dark and vague again, and Evie wanted to shake her out of it. When they'd run home, Mama had been *there*, she had been worried and frightened and panicking, but she had *seen* them. Evie could understand why Mama was shocked. Scarborough was where she and Kitty had gone with her to buy party frocks. It was a town full of beautiful shops and smart tearooms. The Germans couldn't have killed people in *Scarborough*. Evie fixed her eyes on Mama, willing her to hug them again, or to go back to worrying about the shrapnel that had nearly fallen on her daughters. They couldn't let her slip back into her dreamlike grieving.

"I should go and tell the maids," Mama said, pressing her fingertips against her eyes for a moment. "They were worried. The scullery maid was having some sort of . . . fit. Cook was burning feathers under her nose, so the kitchens smell quite unpleasant."

Evie took in a long breath. She didn't think

Mama had noticed any smells, pleasant or not, for months.

Kitty had been very worried that wartime would mean no Christmas presents, but everything seemed to be confusingly the same. The war wasn't over, of course, as a lot of people had said it would be; in fact, it seemed to be only just beginning. Just a week or so after the shells had fallen on Whitby, there were posters everywhere calling for more men to join up. Most of them said REMEMBER SCARBOROUGH. David took Evie and Kitty out to spend some of their Christmas money, and kept on stopping to study them.

"We've seen that one," Kitty moaned, as he stopped again in front of a wall covered in a line of posters. "You're taking ages."

David was standing with his fists clenched, gazing at the picture – a destroyed house, horribly like the one Evie and Kitty had seen on that frantic run home from school. A little girl stood in front of it, holding a baby, and underneath it said:

78 Women & Children
were killed and 228 Women
& Children were wounded
by the German Raiders
ENLIST NOW

"It's not just a poster illustration," David muttered. "This is a real house, number two Wykeham Street in Scarborough. The people who lived here were killed, you know. Two of them were children."

"We do know," Evie pointed out. "We were *here*, actually. The ships that hit Scarborough came here afterwards."

"Yes," David said bitterly. "And I was away at school, probably marching up and down with the OTC in our silly uniforms. While my little sisters nearly got wiped out by shrapnel. Blasted Huns!" He shoved his hands in his pockets and glared at the next poster, which was a figure of Britannia, with a flag and a sword, leading a column of eager men. David's eyes were like theirs, Evie realized – lit up from inside. She grabbed his arm. "Come on. Kitty's getting cross."

David followed her, kicking moodily at the slush that was piled around the streets. He seemed to have been in a bad mood ever since he came back from school, Evie thought. Usually when he was at home he spent most of his time in the attic, where he'd cleared himself a bolthole between the trunks and piles of broken furniture. It was full of books and tubes of paint and tattered sketches. He didn't mind – much – if Evie sneaked up after him and watched him draw, and he'd let her have the back of the paper to draw on herself. This Christmas holiday he'd hardly drawn at all. He'd spent most of his time stretched out on a roll of old carpet, staring at nothing. And he hadn't wanted Evie around at all. He was genuinely furious to have missed "the first exciting thing that's happened in Whitby ever" – and then Kitty had foolishly mentioned the *Rohilla* to him and made it worse, since he had gone to stay with a friend during his half-term and missed that too.

"Look, you two can go and buy sweets by yourselves, can't you?" he said suddenly. "It's not far to the sweet shop, and you know where it is."

"But you're supposed to come with us," Kitty said, stamping her foot. "Mama sent you to. She *said*." She liked walking with David, he was so tall, and they had decided that compared to most of the boys they knew from the boys' side of their school, he was actually quite handsome. Evie had hoped they might meet some of her school friends while they were out, so she could show off her brother.

"Oh, don't be such a baby!" David snapped back. "You walk to school every day by yourselves."

"And what are we supposed to say to Mama when we go back without you?" Evie demanded.

"I don't know! Tell her I met a friend or something. I won't be long, anyway. Look, here's another shilling. Buy me some butterscotch, and you can spend the rest. Go on, Evie, be a sport."

"What are you going to do?" Evie asked him, wrinkling her nose worriedly. David was a reasonably generous older brother, but a shilling? That wasn't like him at all. There was something going on here.

"Don't look like that." David patted her arm in a lordly sort of way. "Just go and spend it, there's a dear."

"Oh!" Kitty stamped her foot again and snatched the shilling. "Go away then, we didn't want you anyway."

"I don't know where he's going," Evie said as David marched away.

"Nor do I, and I don't care." Kitty took her hand and pulled her firmly in the other direction, towards the confectioners.

David wasn't back by the time they got home, laden down with striped paper bags and neat little boxes. He wasn't back by the time they went in to tea, either, and Evie stumbled through an excuse about him remembering something important he had to do. He finally arrived home just after their father came back from the office, looking scared and proud and triumphant all at once.

"I'm not going back to school," he announced, standing in the parlour doorway.

"What?" Daddy blinked at him, and Mama said worriedly, "What do you mean, David? Have you done something wrong? Did you get into trouble? We've heard nothing from the school."

"Of course not. I've joined up." He sauntered into the room and sat down on the arm of a chair, swinging one foot and trying to look relaxed and devil-may-care. And about three years older than he actually was.

"You can't." Kitty was still cross that David had abandoned them. "Don't be stupid. You're far too young to be a soldier."

"Not according to the recruiting office." David shrugged.

"But you are!" Mama surged up out of her chair. "You *are* too young, surely!"

"Eighteen is the recruiting age," their father said, nodding. "So – you lied."

"Only because I want to serve my country!" David's voice shot upwards and he flushed furiously. Most of the time it was low and growling, but just occasionally it still squeaked. It was the only sign that he wasn't eighteen, though. He had always been tall, with huge shoulders, and he had a distinct moustache. He could easily pass as old enough to be a soldier, Evie realized, and the ends of her fingers grew cold with fear. She wrapped them in her skirt and asked, "Does that mean you're going away? You're – you're not going back to school?"

"Of course he's going back to school!" their mother said shrilly. "This is nonsense. I shall go down to the recruiting office and tell them so, tomorrow morning."

"You can't!" David looked horrified. "Mama, you can't, that would be – that would be *awful*."

"How could they be so stupid? How could *you*? Did they not need some kind of proof of your age?"

"I look eighteen, Mama, easily. I'm one of the tallest boys at school. They didn't ask for proof."

"Boys!" She caught her breath, sobbing. "That's all you are. Another one. . ."

"Mama, don't." Evie went to hold her. "It's not the same. David won't go. He won't."

"Yes, I shall," David said determinedly, even though he had turned white. "I'm sorry, Mama, I know it's hard, with Alecky. . . But don't you see? He would have wanted me to go. He would have been proud as anything."

"He was seven!" Mama wailed. "He wouldn't understand. You don't understand, this isn't about marching off with a band playing, and all the girls waving to you. You'll be sent to France, and we'll never get you back again!"

"Helen, don't," Daddy said, gently pushing Evie away and taking Mama's hands. "It was bound to come sooner or later."

"What?" Mama and David said it at the same time, and David sprang up, looking hopeful.

"The war will be over by the time he's old enough," Mama hissed. "It will. It was to be over by Christmas, it can't last much longer. He should be safe at school."

"Perhaps…" Daddy sighed. "But it doesn't seem that way, does it? No one knew what it would be like, not with the weapons we have now. We're entrenched, dug in. It'll go on."

"For years?" Mama whispered.

"It could well last that long. And if David wants to serve… Think of those children in Scarborough, Helen. It could have been Kitty and Evie."

"Exactly!" David nodded eagerly. "How could I stay at home? I have to protect my sisters."

"But it wasn't us," Evie argued, catching his arm. "We're perfectly safe. You might get wounded." She didn't want to say, *Or die*, not in front of Mama, but she thought it.

"You never usually want to protect us anyway!" Kitty added. "You can't call pulling my hair protecting us, can you?"

"Don't, girls. You should be proud of him." Daddy nodded at David, and Evie saw her brother stand straighter, his shoulders back. He looked older and younger at the same time, his mouth set in a stern line, but his eyes sparkling as if he were off for some great treat. She glanced between him and her father, and decided that Daddy looked pleased. Almost envious. She swallowed. "Are you going to join up?"

"I'm too old, Evie. But I've been thinking – they're asking for special constables, to help replace the police who've gone to fight. I may well do that. It's night duty, only every few weeks, so I could manage it with the office."

Mama sat down, looking lost. "I don't understand," she murmured. "How can this be happening? You can't do this, you can't let him go. How *can* you?"

"When do you have to report?" Daddy asked.

"Soon. They'll send a telegram," David explained. "I'll be sent to a training camp first."

*

"Ailsa has a black armband, did you see?" Grace leaned over the table to whisper to the others, and Evie tried to look discreetly behind her.

"Don't all turn round and stare!" Grace rolled her eyes. "Honestly."

"Her father. . . ?" Evie suggested. She wanted to say *brother*, but she couldn't bring herself to ask.

"A brother, more likely," Sybil said, peering round Evie and across the hall.

"She does have one, I've seen him at the concerts and things," Dot agreed.

"Oh," Evie whispered, and she and Grace exchanged a look. They had both agreed that of course they were very proud of their brothers – Grace's was called Harold, and he was in France already – but still. The lists of casualties in the newspapers were so long, and Grace had confided that she hated to see the postman now, in case the letters brought bad news.

David was at his training camp, and seemed to be quite enjoying it. His last letter had said that actually the food was better than he was used to at school. His was a camp for officers, as he had been at a public school, and was supposed to be fit for command. Evie had wondered if this meant that the army would write to the masters at his old school and find out that David was too young, but so far he seemed to be getting away with it, even though there was another boy from Sedburgh there who knew exactly how old he was. Apparently he seemed to think that David had done something very clever, and it was all a grand joke. He wasn't planning to let the secret out.

"Ailsa does seem awfully sad," Evie whispered as she stood up to pile their plates together, and got a chance of another look.

The gossip filtered through the school all afternoon, and by the end of the day, even the Lower Thirds knew that Ailsa's older brother had been killed fighting in France. Evie went home and wrote a letter to David, in which she carefully didn't mention Ailsa's brother.

Dear David,

I see what you meant when you said that the Wars of the Roses were as dry as dust. Miss Bruce, our history mistress, talks about them as though they were all the best fun, but then she is quite strange.

How are you? I hope you received the chocolate Kitty and I sent. Are you allowed to go shopping and buy sweets and things?

I know you are looking forward to going out to France, but I hope the weather improves before you do, as it's horribly wet here.

Max is in disgrace as he has eaten Mama's best hat, which she left on a chair in the parlour. I'm actually surprised that he could reach it, but I think he may have caught it by a trailing ribbon.

With my best love,

Evie

It was a perfectly boring letter, but to Evie every line seemed to be shouting, *Please don't go! Please don't go!*

Chapter Seven

"Mama, what's that?" Evie asked, peering over at the pile of post by her mother's plate. It had been hard to get up that morning, and she felt dazed and sleepy. She had sat up late, writing a letter to David by the faint glow from her candle. She wasn't quite sure why she bothered – he hardly ever wrote back, at least not to her. His excuse was that the training kept them so busy, and he was exhausted. His letters were addressed to Mama, and she passed them round, and even then they were only a few lines, saying that he was well, and thanking everyone for the sweets and chocolate and letters. But when she wrote it felt like a thin, cobweb thread, stretching across the country and tying David to them. Keeping him safe.

The picture card was on top of Mama's letters, and she couldn't quite see it. "Is it an Easter card?" There was a figure in a white dress and it had a religious sort of look, but Easter had been a few weeks before.

"Oh! It's beautiful, isn't it?" Mama smiled at her. "No, darling, Aunt Vivien sent it to me, it's a postcard. She knew I'd want to see it. It's the Angels."

"Not all that again," Daddy muttered. "Absolute nonsense. The fellow who wrote the original newspaper story has said so, Helen, you know that. It was a short story, a piece of fiction, and it was blown up into a mass of sentimental claptrap."

Mama said nothing, only shuffled the papers she was holding, and Daddy sighed and got up. "I'm going down to the office for a while," he said, planting a kiss on her hair. He was working more at weekends now, since he'd started as a special constable. Mama said he was finding it hard to fit everything in, and he was very tired.

Mama murmured goodbye, but that was all, and she didn't get up to go to the door, or fuss about fetching his hat, as she often did. Evie waited until her father had left the room, and then whispered, "Please may I see?" Kitty put down her toast and leaned over to look too.

Mama handed it to Evie, very gently, her fingers stroking the image. "Your father thinks it isn't true, but I'm quite sure that it is, Evie. It makes me feel so much better about David. Someone will be looking after him when he goes out to France, just like this." She nodded to herself, and smiled.

Evie took the card, trying to hold it as carefully as Mama, and studied the picture. Now that she could see it closely, it wasn't quite as pretty as she'd thought. A young man in an infantry uniform stood protecting another soldier with a bloodstained bandage around his head. He was looking down at his rifle, as if he couldn't see that behind him were two tall women in white, with great wings rising above their heads. They were holding swords, and one of them had her hand up, as though she was telling people to stop.

"I don't understand," Evie murmured. "Why did Daddy say it was nonsense?"

Mama sighed. "He doesn't believe in this sort of thing." She took the card back, cradling it in her hands and gazing reverently at the angel figures. "But there were so many witnesses, I don't see how he can say it didn't happen." She gazed seriously at Evie. "It was a miracle, all the soldiers who were there said so."

Evie felt her stomach squirm. Miracles were a church thing – they didn't happen these days. What was Mama talking about?

"And Reverend Allen agrees, you know. He printed the story in the parish magazine." Mama sighed. "I have to keep edging him away from your father on Sundays. I think the night shifts are making Daddy less than patient. . . It's a beautiful story, Evie, I should have told it to you and Kitty before – it'll make you feel better about David too." She patted the chair beside her, smiling eagerly, and as Evie sat down, she slipped an arm around her shoulders. It was like being small again, and Evie leaned gratefully against her. Kitty climbed jealously half into Mama's lap, and smirked.

"It was last August," Mama began, her voice taking on a low storytelling tone, whispered and confiding. "You know, the first great battle that our soldiers faced."

Evie nodded. Only eight months, but it already seemed a long time ago – there had been so many battles reported since.

"The British Expeditionary Force was outnumbered three to one by the Germans, but they had to protect part of the French army – the Germans were coming up behind them and the British force was supposed to keep the Germans away, you see? And they did it. Even though they were so outnumbered, the British threw back the German soldiers, and kept them at bay for two days – it was incredible." Mama shook her head. "But then things took a turn for the worse, and they were about to be overrun by the enemy. One of our soldiers prayed for help. He was desperate, so he called on St George – and the saint came."

"St George?" Evie wriggled, trying to look up at her. St George was centuries old, from back when there were dragons. And actually, dragons were only a fairy tale thing, which made St George a bit doubtful too. There was a fairy tale feel to this whole story, the way Mama was telling it.

"Yes, St George and a legion of shining bowmen! They filled in the gap in the line, and fought the Germans back."

"Oh, Mama. . ." Kitty began, shaking her head.

"It's true." Mama sighed. "You're far too much like your father, Kitty. Have a little faith. The soldiers described it afterwards, so many of them saw! And there were bodies of German soldiers on the battlefield, marked with arrow wounds," she added impressively. "The bowmen were the famous archers who turned the tide at the Battle of Agincourt. They came back to fight and save our poor soldiers."

"Oh. . ." Evie thought of David, and his cheerful scraps of letters, illustrated with portraits of the boys in the training camp. How wonderful to think that someone was looking after him. It was true that Mr Allen had said in several of his sermons that God would of course be on the side of the British, after the horrific way that the Germans had treated the Belgian refugees, and their prisoners of war. Miracles had happened once; why not again, if the need was desperate enough? "But – these have swords, not bows," she added, pointing to the card.

"No, well. . . That's what your father was talking about. The man who first reported the bowmen tried to claim later that the whole story was only something he'd made up, I don't know why. But since then so many other soldiers have come forward to say that it's true, they did see something. Some of them said it was a huge, glowing cloud, and others described angels who'd helped them to escape from the German forces. It's clearer and clearer that some heavenly force was on their side that day, even if it was hard to describe."

"Those angels don't have any feet," Kitty said critically, examining the card.

"Angels float, Kitty!" Evie snapped. She wanted there to be an angel, hovering behind David – and Mama looked so sure, so happy as she stared at the card. Was it enough, just to *need* it to be true?

"I can't," Kitty said crossly. "Miss Bell sent back my arithmetic all covered in red ink, and now I have to do it again, before tomorrow. You'll have to walk the dogs by yourself." She leaned down and stroked the curls of Brandy's little beard. "Ugh, you're dribbling," she told him fondly. "I hate arithmetic, Evie."

Evie, who had discovered since going to the County School that she was actually much better at maths than she thought she was, nodded sympathetically. She didn't want to make Kitty any more bad-tempered. "Perhaps it won't take as long as you think," she suggested. "We can play badminton in the garden when I'm back. It's light till so much later now."

"It's too hot," Kitty growled.

Evie leaned over the crumpled-looking exercise book and looked at Kitty's scruffy prep. "The second one's wrong," she said apologetically, and made for the door before Kitty found anything to throw at her.

It was rather nice to be without Kitty, she thought to herself as she and the dogs threaded their way along the dusty streets to the clifftop path. With no complaining from her little sister, she could walk along the West Cliff and nearly as far as Sandsend, she thought. Well, perhaps not that far, since it was so hot, but a good distance.

Brandy trotted on ahead while Max pulled hard at his lead. He was sure he should be allowed to run free too, but Evie had wasted too many hours chasing him up the beach to let him try. He was awful at coming when he was called, he would just run and run, ears flapping. The stretch of open space along the cliff path would send him galloping, Evie knew it, and even though he was little, he had a surprising turn of speed.

"Heel, Max!" she said sternly, and the little dachshund looked up at her for a moment and then set off again, pulling just as hard.

"You'll choke yourself," Evie sighed as he surged towards an interesting bit of wall, and then started making strangled gobbling noises against his collar. An old lady walking by on the other side of the street stared at her disapprovingly, and Evie ducked her head and hurried on, tugging Max after her. "Honestly," she whispered. "You should have seen the look she was giving me! Why do you always get me into trouble?"

Brandy circled back to check on them, herding Max and Evie on. The cliff path stretched ahead of them completely empty, and Evie let Max's lead hang a little looser, so he could explore and sniff about. It was too hot for fast walking, she decided dreamily as she dawdled along. The dogs were happy not to go too fast either.

The rough grass along the path was full of wild flowers, and there were bees humming, and butterflies. Evie wished she'd brought a sketchbook and paints to capture some of the colours – but the dogs would never have sat still long enough to let her. She was watching a small Peacock butterfly swooping around a patch of gorse when she heard voices coming up the path behind her. Hastily, she tugged on Max's lead to bring him back closer, in case the walkers had a dog with them. She didn't want him running up to another dog and yapping – he couldn't be made to understand that he was small, and he was quite unafraid of even the hugest dog.

The voices belonged to a group of boys, a little

older than Evie, dressed in knitted pullovers and flat caps. She supposed they were on their way to one of the villages, and drew back off the path to be out of their way – they were walking much faster than she was.

They touched their caps to her as they went past, and looked admiringly at Brandy, who was standing next to Evie, alert and watchful.

"Grand dog, that, miss," one of them said, and Evie smiled at him and nodded. Then Max bounced out of the long grass, where he'd been chasing a bumblebee, and landed on the path by Evie's feet, tail wagging and eager.

The lads laughed, but then the closest one crouched down to look better at Max. Then he stood up, towering over Evie, and said grimly, "One o'them Hun dogs. A dachshund, tha's it. Why's tha got a German dog, miss?"

Brandy moved to stand between Evie and the boy, letting out a low, warning growl, but the boy ignored him.

"He – he's not German. He came from a lady in Redcar," Evie faltered, looking around and hoping for another walker to come along the path and tell the boys to leave her alone.

"Filthy Germans," one of the others yelled. "Killed a thousand on that ship last week. Is tha a German, then, lass?"

"No!" Evie squeaked. "Of course not! I live here."

"Littl' Hun spy."

"No, I'm not, go away! Leave us alone!"

All this time Brandy had been growling and showing his teeth at the boys, while Max stared up at them in confusion. He wasn't used to strangers shouting at him – he was usually petted and made a fuss of when they went out walking. He huddled back towards Evie and waved his tail nervously.

Then one of the boys made a grab for him, and Max darted away, whimpering, so that Evie stumbled across the path. Brandy snarled and leaped at the boy, seizing a part of his jacket in his teeth, while the boy swore and hit at him, trying to knock him away, and the others surged around them.

"Brandy, no!" Evie wailed. If Brandy hurt them, what would they do? They were so angry now, all of them. They might hit him properly hard, and one of the boys had a stick.

Brandy fell away, whining, as the boy managed to catch him a clip around the head, and then laughed wildly as the others egged him on. His face was flushed scarlet, and he'd lost his cap. There was a great rent in his jacket where Brandy had worried at it. "Ah'm gonna throw yon Hun dog off t'cliff!" he shouted, and he dived for Max, grabbing hold of the puppy's collar and lifting him up, so he wriggled and howled, his eyes bulging.

"No!" Evie screamed, and she grabbed at Max too, dragging the boy back away from the edge with one hand and snatching desperately at her dog with the other. The cliffs weren't as steep here as they were on the east side of the town, but she knew that if the boy flung Max down, he was bound to be hurt. The fall might even kill him. It might kill *her*, if she slipped over the edge and hit her head on a rock, she thought, as they scrabbled and fought on the slippery grass.

"Arthur! Let 'er be!" yelled one of the others behind them. "Tha'll knock t'lass over, and us'll be in bother."

"Tha's soft," the boy holding Max sneered. "Run off home, then, if tha's afeared." He shook Max, and the puppy squealed again in fright and pain.

That last terrified scream was enough for Brandy and Evie both. Evie snatched up a stone from the path, ready to throw it at the boy – she didn't care if he was hurt, not if he could be so cruel. But it was so hard to aim when she mustn't risk hitting Max.

As she stood hesitating for a moment, Brandy came up beside her. The Airedale seemed to have worked out that he couldn't jump from the path without knocking the boy and Max down the slope. Instead he crept carefully past Evie and launched himself at the boy from the edge of the cliff, his back paws scrabbling for a second on the thin grass that led down the slope. The other boys were all looking at the squirming puppy, and didn't notice him getting ready to spring. They'd already hit him, and perhaps they thought that he was too dazed to keep on fighting. To Evie it seemed as though a hissing, black-and-tan bomb had suddenly exploded next to her, and she fell back for a moment, gasping.

The boy landed on his side on the path, cursing furiously, and with Brandy on his back, growling menacingly into his ear. The shock of the fall had made the boy drop Max, who lay wheezing miserably next to him, until Evie scooped him up in her arms, his lead dangling. "Brandy, come!" she screamed, and raced back along the path towards the town while the boys were crowded around their ringleader, who was lying on the ground.

She ran as fast as she could, not sure if the boys

were chasing after her. Max was horribly quiet in her arms, but she didn't dare stop to see if he was hurt. Brandy bounded along beside her, but she could see that there was a cut just above his eye, and blood was seeping into his crinkled fur.

At last they reached the edges of the town, where there were houses built along the top of the cliff, and benches for walkers to rest and look out to sea. Panting and stumbling, Evie dared to slow down at last. She looked back over her shoulder, but there was no sign of the gang of boys. She sank down on to the first bench and gently patted Max's head. The dachshund puppy whined, looking up at her with woeful black eyes. Nothing like this had ever happened in his whole young life, and he huddled against her, shaking. Brandy sat down on Evie's feet, looking smug.

"I hope you knocked that boy out," she said viciously, reaching down one hand to stroke him. "You poor darling. We'll get you home, and put a cold cloth on your eye."

She leaned back against the bench, feeling suddenly sick. All the fear and panic and fury that she'd bottled up on the cliff seemed to hit her at once, and she made a strange high whimpering noise that had both dogs up on their feet and eyeing her anxiously. Max climbed up her front, his little ginger forepaws on her shoulders, and nudged a damp nose to her cheek, and Brandy jumped up on to the bench next to her and growled, as if promising to fight off any more toughs that might appear.

"What am I going to say at home?" Evie whispered shakily to them. "I'll have to tell them what happened – your eye's cut, and my blouse sleeve is torn. Mama will probably say we can't ever walk on our own again. But I never meant for it to happen – I mean, we didn't do anything wrong. And you're not a Hun dog," she added angrily, wrapping her arms around Max's warm sausage body. The solid weight of him cuddled against her made Evie feel a little calmer, and Max whipped his thin tail back and forth and licked her cheek. He seemed to be recovering,

"I suppose we should go back home," Evie said, drawing a shuddering breath. "Before those evil boys catch up with us." She looked anxiously down the path, but there was still no one coming. Perhaps the boys assumed she would have run to fetch help, and had scattered back along the path. She got up carefully, not entirely sure that the wobbly feeling had gone, and put Max down on the grass. He whined and held up one paw, gazing up at her tragically.

"Oh!" Evie crouched down beside him and felt the paw, moving it gently to and fro. There didn't seem to be anything wrong with it at all, and Max didn't flinch when she touched him. "Are you just faking because you want me to keep on carrying you, little rotter?"

Max beat his tail on the grass but continued to look soulful, and Evie sighed and picked him up again. "Sorry, Brandy," she said, looking down at the Airedale. "You're too heavy, even though I think you're far more hurt than he is."

She felt stiff and tired now, and her torn blouse and dusty tunic attracted several odd glances as she walked back through the town to home. When two women she was sure she knew from church – or perhaps they were friends of Mama's? – glared at her in horror, Evie felt tears burning behind her eyes. It wasn't fair.

She went in through the side passage, which she and Kitty quite often did; it wasn't really that she was trying to hide. . . But it was no use anyway. She was trying to wash the dust off her hands – and her face, which she now saw was covered too – when Sarah found her in the scullery.

"Miss Evie, those dogs have left dust all over the clean tiles – wha happened, lass?" She twitched at the sleeve of Evie's blouse, and then saw the smear of dirt down her cheek. "Didst tha fall?"

Evie shook her head. "These awful boys, they

chased us. Because Max is a dachshund – they called him a Hun dog."

Max heard his name and looked up at Sarah, wagging his tail doubtfully. She had been known to chase him with a broom.

"Littl' beggars." Sarah scowled. "Best go and change, and bring me that blouse to mend."

Evie nodded. If she was clean and tidy before she encountered Mama, there was more chance she'd be able to pass the encounter off as a minor squabble. She trailed up the stairs from the basement and peeped through into the hall. She could hear Mama talking to someone in the parlour, and she prepared to nip quickly past and hurry up to her room.

"Evie! You look a little scarecrow, child, what have you been doing?"

Evie whirled round, and realized that her father had been standing by the front door, taking off his hat. She'd been too busy watching for Mama to notice.

"What's happened?" Mama appeared at the parlour door and sighed disapprovingly. "Oh, Evie!"

"What did you do to Brandy?" Kitty squealed, following Mama out and crouching down to look at Brandy's cut head. "Did you fall down the cliff?" she added, obviously hoping for drama.

"No!" But they almost had. Evie shuddered.

"Are you hurt? Evie, what happened to the dog?" Daddy took her arm to pull her into the light streaming through the doorway, and Evie caught her breath. She hadn't realized that the boys had bruised her.

"Evie, were you *fighting*?" Mama's voice rose in shock, and Evie shook her head hurriedly.

"No! Well, I suppose yes, but not because I wanted to." Max was whimpering again at all the raised voices, and she pulled away from her father and bent down wearily to pick him up. "We were walking along the cliff path – Kitty couldn't come because she had prep to do – and some boys—"

"Which boys?" her father snapped. "Did you know them?"

"No . . . I suppose they were fisherboys, they had ganseys on, a couple of them." Evie tried to think. Yes, they'd mostly had on dark knitted pullovers, the kind all the local fishermen wore, apart from the boy who'd seized Max. He was the only one wearing an old wool jacket. "They were just walking past, they even said what a nice dog Brandy was. But then they saw Max, and they got so angry."

"Oh, God. . ." Evie's father groaned. "I suppose we should have expected it. But here? I mean, there were riots in London and Manchester, windows smashed on German shops. I never thought it would happen in Whitby, even with all the anger about the sinking of the *Lusitania*."

Evie nodded. "The boy said that," she said, her voice very small. It was frightening, seeing her father so upset. She had expected them to be cross with her, not this. "He said a thousand people died. He tried to throw Max down the cliff."

"Oh!" Mama pressed her hand to her mouth.

"And – and they said I was a German spy," Evie whispered. "That I was a Hun too." There was a silence, and she went on desperately. "I *told* them he came from Redcar."

Her father half laughed, but it was a bitter, worried sound. He looked at Max, cuddled in Evie's arms, and then turned away, starting to pace up and down the hall. His boot-heels clicked on the patterned tiles, and the little sound seemed to echo in the silent house. Evie watched him, and felt sick again. She was more scared now than she had been when the boys had been fighting to grab Max, and she didn't know why.

At last, her father turned back and sighed. "We'll have to get rid of him."

"What?" Evie said disbelievingly.

"I can't be seen to be unpatriotic, Evie. It would be very bad for business."

"But – but you're a lawyer," Evie stammered. "That's nothing to do with dogs. Or Germans."

163

"It seems rather extreme, Charles," Mama put in. "I mean, a little puppy. How could anyone possibly think. . ."

"The feeling in the country *is* extreme," he said grimly. "There have been riots in London, Liverpool. All the cities. There was forty thousand pounds' worth of damage done in Liverpool, Helen! Any form of sympathy with the Germans is suspect at once. And that dog is German."

Evie hugged Max tighter. "You can't get rid of him," she said, her voice shaking. "He isn't yours, he's mine. He was mine for my birthday. It would be stealing, if you tried to take him away." Then she added, "And what would you do with him? If he's a German dog and no one wants him. . ." She trailed off, and gazed at her father in horror. "You wouldn't!"

He glanced away from her uneasily.

"You can't, Charles!" Mama came to Evie's side, and put a hand on her shoulder. "I won't let you. You're taking this too far."

164

"Of course I don't want to!" Evie's father exploded. "But I can't see any other way. Besides, now the U-boats are attacking shipping, the food shortages are only going to get worse. It will be difficult to feed a dog. I'm only being sensible."

"Sensible about what?" Kitty asked, looking between them all. "I don't understand."

"He says *get rid* of Max, but he means he's going to drown him," Evie told her. "Or poison him. I don't know."

"Poison! Of course not," her father said crossly. "Don't be ridiculous."

"You can't!" Kitty looked horrified. "I thought you meant you'd send him somewhere nice. Like those kittens that the kitchen cat at the house next door had. They sent them to a farm."

Evie sighed, but Mama shook her head and gave her a warning look, so she didn't say anything. Mama was on her side, for now.

"Daddy thinks a farm wouldn't want him because of being German," she explained. "But saying it's because of feeding him is just silly," she added, realizing this suddenly, and turning back to scowl at him. "Max is tiny, and he's always going to be tiny. Brandy eats twice as much, are you going to *send him away* too?"

"Besides, David adores Max," Mama said firmly. "What would he say if he came home on leave and found him gone?"

Evie bit her lip. She didn't think David liked Max all that much – but he had said in his letters that he liked to think of them all at home, hadn't he? He would be imagining Max there, curled on Evie's lap, and Brandy lying on the hearthrug in front of the nursery fire, with Kitty stretched out next to him. The dogs were in the photograph of Kitty and Evie that their father had taken to send to David. "We have to keep everything the same," said Evie pleadingly. "We *have* to. And if you drown Max just because he has a German name, that's an atrocity, like the Germans killing those children on the *Lusitania*."

"Evie!" Her father sounded furious. "How can you say such a thing? You have no idea what you're talking about, no idea at all. Go to your room! And take that dratted creature with you." But he didn't stay to watch her go. He strode away to his study, and Mama and Evie and Kitty stared after him, and flinched as he slammed the door.

He went off like that because he didn't know what to say, Evie thought in surprise. *Mama argued with him, and so did I, and I was* right.

Chapter Eight

No one mentioned getting rid of Max again, but Evie couldn't forget the way her father had looked at the little dog. She had been worried that she would get into trouble, that she would be banned from walking the dogs, but it had been far worse. Something that she had always depended on seemed to have gone. After Alecky had died, she and Kitty had gradually understood that Mama was fragile, maybe even a little broken. They had crept around her, and fussed over her, and tried not to make her cry, even though she often still did.

But Daddy had been strong and calm and sensible. He knew about things. He read the newspapers, and told them what was happening in France. He played golf with the chief constable, or he had before the war, and he went out and guarded things at night with the other specials.

He didn't drown dogs.

She and Kitty made ribbon rosettes, red, white and blue, and sewed them on to Max's collar. He kept trying to chew them, so they never lasted for very long, but it was better than nothing, and quite a few people stopped them to admire him when they were out. Even Mr Allen, the vicar, smiled at him, and told Evie that it was a very sensible idea, and perhaps they should add a little Union Jack. He muttered to himself, and patted his pockets, and at last produced a flag day flag, a battered wisp of silk. "I knew I had one somewhere," he said, handing it to Kitty. "Be careful of the pin. There are so many flag days, and one can't wear them all. Poor little thing," he added, looking at Max, and then at the girls with his head on one side. "Have you had trouble?"

"Some boys tried to throw him off the cliff!" Kitty said impressively.

Mr Allen shook his head. "I suppose I shouldn't be surprised." He pulled a little notebook out of his pocket and scribbled in it with a pencil. "Persecution of innocents. Sermon notes," he explained to the curious girls. "One should always be ready."

Evie listened hopefully for several weeks afterwards, but she wasn't sure that Max's collar ever made it into a sermon. Still, telling Daddy about the flag seemed to make him frown at Max a little less. He might not trust Mr Allen's views on Angels, but the vicar was extremely respectable, and respectable was what mattered.

The War Aid Committee was still knitting, although it seemed rather an anticlimax after their triumphant fundraising for Princess Mary's Christmas Gift, and its dramatic end. One

Saturday morning in June, Evie and Kitty went down to the shop in Flowergate with Grace again. David had been home on leave but had left again the week before, as his battalion was being sent out to France, so it was good to be distracted.

"Why on earth are you wearing that?" Evie said as soon as Grace came down her front steps.

Grace put her shoulders back and set the tin hat straight on her head. "Zepps," she said. "You never know when there might be one overhead."

"Zeppelins only come at night," Evie pointed out.

Grace shook her head. "Not always. And they bombed Hull, you know. Hull isn't all that far from here."

Evie chewed her lip. It was true. She had read a newspaper account of the attack, and it sounded terrifying – huge cigar-shaped airships suddenly appearing out of the darkness, and raining down bombs.

"The attack on Hull was an accident, Daddy

said so," Kitty told Grace. "They were aiming for London and they got blown off course. Pretty awful aim."

"I'm not going out with you in a tin hat, Grace," Evie said, imagining what the clerks in the wool shop would be whispering. "You look *idiotic*."

Grace sighed. "It *is* a little bit big."

"And I don't know what good a tin hat would be if you were hit by a bomb anyway."

"It was for debris!" Grace protested. "Like on the playing field. Oh, just give me a minute. It's awfully uncomfortable anyway." She dashed back inside and came out a few moments later in a pretty flower-trimmed straw hat that Evie envied. It was much more grown up than anything Mama would allow her to wear.

"There, satisfied?" Grace twirled in front of them, showing it off, and they walked down the road to Flowergate. After they had bought the knitting wool, they wandered further along the road, arguing lazily about where to go next. Evie fancied going on down to the harbour, to look at the boats and spy on the fishergirls crowded along the harbour rails, gossiping and knitting. Kitty wanted more shopping time, she was planning to spend her pocket money on dolls' house furniture. Grace was trying to persuade her to give the money to the Blind Soldiers' Fund instead and make chairs out of pins and conkers, when Evie shook Grace's arm and said, "What are they doing?"

"Who?" Grace looked round. "Oh. I don't know."

Up ahead of them were three girls, a good bit older than Evie and Grace, perhaps the age of Elaine and Ailsa. They were smartly dressed, but in their hands they held bunches of white feathers.

"They look as if they've been plucking chickens," Kitty said, staring.

The girls seemed to be arguing with two young men, holding out the feathers and gesturing with them, as though they wanted the men to take them. Both the men were trying to edge away, but a small crowd had gathered behind them, laughing and pointing, and they were cut off.

"You're cowards!" one of the girls said dramatically, and the crowd behind the men booed and whistled.

"You should join up at once," another of the girls said, as she leaned over and tried to stick a feather in the man's jacket lapel. He dodged back, and there was a chorus of laughs and jeers. The three girls were giggling, and clearly enjoying having an audience.

"Is it to show they aren't soldiers?" Kitty asked Evie.

"I suppose so, but I don't know why it's white feathers."

"There's a book, I think," Grace said vaguely. "About feathers. I say, what a grand idea. Why should they loaf around here, when my brother and yours are fighting in France? It's disgusting!" And she hissed loudly, and made Evie jump.

Evie nodded slowly. Both the young men looked

so embarrassed, and she felt rather sorry for them, shamed so in front of a crowd, but Grace was right. It didn't seem fair that they hadn't joined up. Grace had shown them her brother's last letter, where he'd mentioned being "a bit tired" and had said he'd been taken back behind the lines for a "rest-cure". Evie had read that part over and over, wondering what it really meant. *She* was a bit tired, waking up early when the bright sun shone in through her bedroom curtains. She was pretty sure that wasn't what Harold meant. And soon it would be happening to David too.

"Beasts," she muttered, meaning the two young men, and Kitty stuck her fingers in her mouth and whistled shrilly. Evie and Grace turned round to stare at her, and she went pink. "Jack who does the garden taught me," she muttered. And then, "He's joining up as soon as he can, he said so."

Evie nodded. Everyone was doing their bit – even Mama was out several evenings each week now, knitting, or helping to roll bandages, or learning first aid. She still worried endlessly about David, who would be in France any day, but the worrying seemed to have stung her into action.

"I wish I was old enough to go and do something," Grace muttered. "I could drive an ambulance, or work as a nurse. Except blood makes me feel sick, but I bet I could try."

Evie nodded. Everyone at school was the same, eager to do something – anything – for the war effort. How could anyone not believe in fighting, when their country was in such danger? And every other young man around was in khaki?

Then she frowned, and took a couple of steps closer. The men were still dodging the girls with the feathers, and trying to protest, and she had just realized that one of them looked familiar.

"Kitty, isn't that Frank? Daddy's clerk, you know? We saw him when we went to meet Daddy at the office."

Kitty looked at the two men with her head on

one side. "The one with the pale hair?" she asked thoughtfully.

"Yes, don't you remember? He was very nice, he gave us peppermint humbugs while we were waiting for Daddy."

Kitty brightened. "Oh, yes. They were very good humbugs – they were enormous." She looked sadly at Evie. "I would have thought someone as nice as him would *want* to go and fight for his country."

"Yes, but that's what I'm trying to say." Evie nodded firmly. "He did. I'm sure he did – and he went out to France quickly too, because he was already in the Territorials and knew lots about being a soldier. I remember Daddy saying so, because he hired that lady clerk instead and he was worried about it. He told Mama that her typing was very good, but that she wore her hair in a way that he didn't think was at all appropriate for the office."

"What was wrong with it?" Grace asked curiously.

"I don't know! It was different from Mama's, I suppose. But it doesn't matter anyway – that's

Frank, and he *is* a soldier. They shouldn't be trying to call him a coward. I expect he's a very good soldier."

"Oh! Yes." Grace looked back at Frank with more interest. "Why doesn't he tell them?"

"They aren't listening," Evie pointed out. "And he's too polite to yell at them."

Just then, the other young man suddenly managed to dart past the girls with the feathers, and away up a side street, leaving Frank facing all three girls, and all the attention of the crowd. An elderly man spat at his feet and shouted, "Tha should be shamed, a gurt lad laik thee! Three grandsons, ah've got, all o' them over t'water fighting!"

"But – but—" Frank turned round, obviously wanting to explain to the old man, and there was a barrage of cheers as one of the girls saw that he was distracted and managed to stick a white feather in his buttonhole. Frank stared down at it in horror, and shook his head.

Kitty sighed disgustedly and marched forward, pushing her way between Frank and the girls. "You great stupid," she shouted at him. "Why didn't you just say?" The crowd stared, and then cheered again – unsure what was happening, but enjoying the show. Kitty plucked the feather from Frank's jacket and held it out to the girl who'd put it there. "He *is* a soldier already! You ought to listen! I expect he's on leave."

"I was sent home injured," the young man muttered.

"There, you see! He was injured fighting for his country!" Kitty nodded, and the girl looked sulky.

"Well, he could have said." She took the feather back and stared down at it rather crossly. She didn't look nearly as embarrassed as Evie felt she ought to.

"Where were you hurt?" Kitty asked, and Frank stared at her.

"I was shot in the leg, miss," he murmured.

The crowd were breaking up now, wandering

away and leaving the three girls looking pink and flustered. Frank nodded to Kitty, lifted his hat and hurried away – he did have a very noticeable limp, Evie saw.

"Well! He might have said thank you," Kitty said indignantly. "But then I suppose he was upset. You ought to have checked," she added in a righteous voice, staring at the girl who'd given him the feather.

"Mind your own business!" the girl snapped, and she turned with a flounce, shooing her two companions along the street to avoid the last muttering bystanders.

"Kitty! I don't know how you dared!" Grace giggled. "With all those people watching."

"She never cares what anyone thinks," Evie said gloomily. "Haven't you worked that out by now?"

"We couldn't just leave him to be white-feathered," Kitty pointed out. "It wasn't fair! If those girls can't tell who's a soldier and who isn't, they shouldn't go around picking on people."

180

Chapter Nine

Evie sat bundled up in the wicker chair in the nursery, with Max asleep on her lap and a shawl wrapped around her head. They had gone from a horrible rainy summer to a horrible rainy winter, and she had a cold. Brandy was lying on her feet and keeping them warm, but he looked up as he heard footsteps thundering on the stairs.

"You'll never guess what's happened!" Kitty burst into the room.

"What?" Evie snuffled, and Brandy heaved

himself up with a sigh to greet Kitty. "Oh, he was the only thing stopping me turning into an icicle."

"Never mind, I can sit on your feet." Kitty curled up next to her and hugged her ankles while Brandy watched disapprovingly, clearly feeling that floors were for dogs. "Lizzie and Mary-Ann are leaving!"

"What?" Evie struggled a little further out of the nest of scarves and blankets that made her look like a tortoise. "Why? I know Mama and Mrs Dixon are always complaining about Mary-Ann smashing the good china, but I thought Mama said that maids were like hen's teeth? And what did Lizzie do?"

"Nothing." Kitty shook her head. "Mama hasn't sacked them, they've given notice, both of them. They're leaving together to work in a munitions factory."

Evie shook her head. "They can't. Mama won't let them."

"They are going to, and think about it, Evie. Mama can't tell them they mustn't, it's war work. It would be unpatriotic. Though she did offer them a raise to try and persuade them to stay."

"And they're still going?"

"The factory pays a lot more." Kitty sighed. "Mrs Dixon is furious. She's clashing pans around like anything."

Evie tried to think of all the things that Lizzie and Mary-Ann did. The washing up, for a start. That was Mary-Ann's main job, as the scullery maid, that and preparing vegetables. Was Mrs Dixon going to have to do all that herself now? No wonder she was cross. Lizzie was the second housemaid. She and Sarah between them did all the bedrooms every morning, made the fires, dusted, swept, polished, and helped the weekly washerwoman with the laundry. And Sarah helped lady's maid Mama when there was a special occasion. Not that there were many of those, just now.

"What will we do?" Evie muttered. They *needed* Lizzie and Mary-Ann. Although she supposed the country needed them more.

"Mama's drafting an advertisement now," Kitty told her. "But I'm not sure she'll find anyone. I'd rather go and work in a factory than be a scullery maid, wouldn't you?"

"Maybe." There had been photographs of munitionettes in the newspapers, and it looked like an exhausting job. The girls had to haul around huge shells, and some of them were working next to enormous clattering machines, or with dangerous chemicals. Then again, Mary-Ann's hands were already scarlet and chapped from the hot water and soda, and she had Mrs Dixon shouting at her most of the day. Perhaps a factory would be more fun. "I'm not sure. Do you think Lizzie and Mary-Ann will turn yellow? Like those canary girls Mama told us about?"

"Lizzie said to Mrs Dixon that she didn't care if the TNT did turn her yellow," Kitty reported. "The factory pays half as much again as her wages from us. Are you going to stay up here all day?"

"I'm ill!"

"If Mama can't get more maids, do you think we'll have to make our own beds, and carry the coal up the stairs and light the fires?" Kitty sighed. "You won't have time to be ill. Not with helping in the garden as well."

They stared at each other, half horrified and half excited. Jack, the boy who did most of the heavy work in the garden, had told their father a couple of months before that he had finished digging up the long flower bed for a vegetable garden, and he'd planted potatoes and onions and beetroot for winter harvesting. Everyone was being encouraged to grow vegetables, now that the German U-boats were stopping ships bringing food from overseas. The parks had all been dug up for potatoes, and now families were digging up their flower gardens too. But Jack wouldn't be there to harvest the veg he'd planted, he'd explained, twisting his cap in his hands. He had volunteered, and would be going off to a training camp in a week or so. Mr Maitland had only sighed, and nodded, and then he tipped

Jack a shilling to go and buy himself a pint and some cigarettes to celebrate. He had explained to Evie and Kitty that they would have to help him look after the garden – which wasn't particularly enticing, since it seemed to have been raining for ever and the lawn was a sea of mud. So far all they'd had to do was hoeing, and earthing up the potatoes, neither of which were very difficult, but took ages. Kitty had told Mrs Dixon that she'd quite happily give up potatoes, if it would help.

Evie reckoned that the best way to dig the potatoes up when the time came would be to train Max to do it for them. Dachshunds were bred to dig out badgers, after all. A few potatoes couldn't be too hard. Then again, she thought, looking at Max, who had gone back to sleep on her lap, he didn't give the impression that he would be very keen to work. He was lying on his back half under her blanket, with all his paws in the air and his ears spilling backwards, making tiny whiffling snores.

The first day without Lizzie and Mary-Ann, Sarah woke the girls as she always did, but their bedrooms were cold.

"I haven't time for fires up here, Miss Evie, not with Cook needing help with t'breakfast. Just dress thysen and hurry down."

"We'll freeze," Kitty muttered as Evie brushed her hair. "It's cruel, making us dress up here. There's frost on the *inside* of my window!"

"Miss Speirs doesn't approve of fires in bedrooms," Evie said, remembering a wet day health lecture from the gym mistress. "She says they're insanitary. And we should sleep with the windows open."

Kitty shuddered dramatically. "No, thank you."

Breakfast was decidedly less generous than usual, and the girls' father poked grimly at the chafing dishes on the sideboard.

"Cook simply can't provide such an elaborate breakfast now," Mama was explaining as the girls came in. "Kedgeree is quite time-consuming to prepare, Charles! There are kippers, won't they do?"

"Ugh." Kitty wrinkled her nose at Evie. "Is there bacon?"

"*Yes*, Kitty." Mama sighed. "There is bacon. But please remember that we are supposed to be frugal. We mustn't waste food. The high prices are having a dreadful effect on some families, so the vicar was telling me; they can't even afford to buy enough bread now that the flour shortages have sent the price up so much. Children are going hungry. And just imagine what poor David is having for breakfast."

"Those army biscuits, probably." Evie nodded. "He said in his last letter that his friend Arthur broke his front tooth biting into one." David seemed to be getting better at writing home now he was actually in France. His letters were always short, but he did at least write separately to her and Kitty, instead of stingily palming them off with letters to Mama. His letters were often rather funny, although Evie suspected he was leaving a lot out.

"I don't want to waste food," Kitty said, getting up to help herself to bacon. "I want to *eat* it. I'm ravenous. It's probably because I'm chilled to the bone," she added pathetically.

"You can have a fire in your room, Kitty," Daddy said, dissecting his kipper, and Kitty brightened up. "If you carry up the coal, lay the fire, light it, and then clean the grate." He sighed, and waved a kipper-laden fork at her. "You'll probably have to sweep the chimney too. I expect the sweep's on his way to Belgium."

"I was only saying," Kitty muttered sulkily.

"You can have extra blankets," Mama said, and Kitty and Evie exchanged a worried look, thinking it was quite likely they'd given the extra blankets away after the shipwreck.

"I suppose dugouts are awfully cold too," Kitty murmured, sighing.

Chapter Ten

27 December 1915

Dearest Evie,

    Thank you for the socks. I don't mind at all that one is longer than the other, they're good and thick, which is what matters. Wet feet are the worst thing about being out here, after the food, of course.

    Cheerio,

    David

27 December 1915

Dearest Kitty,

Thank you for the wither pad. As you say, I don't have a horse, but I'm sure I can find one that will be grateful. It's very Christmassy. Was the sugar meant for the horse too? If so, very sorry, as I put it in my tea. All our tea tastes of soup because soup and tea are made in the same vat, so I needed it more than any horse did.

Love,

David

20 January 1916

Dearest David,

Yes, of course the sugar was for the horse! But never mind. I have sent you some peppermints. Half are for you and half are for any horses you come across. Horses are very fond of mint. I hope the war is going well.

Love from Kitty

26 February 1916

Dearest David,

I suppose there will be many more soldiers
now that there is conscription, and everyone who
is old enough must join up. Do you not think this
means the war will be over soon, and you can
come home? Mama is looking quite cheerful, I
think she hopes so.

Have you had snow? School has been closed as
nobody could get anywhere, we've had so much.
Kitty has chilblains and blames the snow and is
cross all the time, but I love it. Everything looks
so different. I found the old sledge up in the attic
and persuaded Kitty to sledge down the hill with
me, it was topping. Brandy adores digging in the
snow, and keeps finding sticks and being very
proud of himself, but Max is much like Kitty. I
don't think dogs get chilblains, but he's so low to
the ground that he only has to step outside and
he's soaked. I tried to dig him a tunnel out into
the garden, but a bit of it collapsed and since then

he has refused to go out at all. His badger-hunting relatives would be ashamed.

Best love,

Evie

15 March 1916
Dearest Evie,

Yes, we have had snow too. Very strange to see the ground ahead of us, which I know to be full of craters and wire, softened to such clean, smooth whiteness. Horribly cold, of course, and the mud in our trenches is awful. Our batman is jolly clever and has built us a fireplace out of a biscuit tin of all things. We have been issued with sheepskin coats and some rather odd-looking gumboots, but still getting sick of everything being so damp. We are only about twenty yards from Fritz and friends here, so it's rather busy, as you can guess. Must sign off now.

Much love,

David

PS Please tell Kitty no, sorry, I cannot send her a photograph of the horse.

5 April, 1916
Dearest David,

I have told Kitty to shut up about the horse. (Did you actually find a horse to give that crocheted monstrosity to? I don't expect the poor thing will be grateful, but she would insist on sending it. It's taken her more than a year to finish it, and she was absurdly proud.)

Twenty yards! That seems awfully close. Please write back soon and tell us that you are safe.

The junior netball team played St Hilda's juniors yesterday, a very even game all round, but we beat them by two goals in the end. Miss Speirs said that I was a credit to the team, but Dot tripped over in the middle of the game and has sprained her wrist horribly. Of course it's the right one, so she is sitting there in class like a duchess while everyone takes notes for her.

Much love,

Evie

29 April 1916

Dearest Evie,

DO NOT SHOW THIS LETTER TO KITTY.
Tell her it's about her birthday or something.
(When is her birthday?)

All right, I didn't give the wither pad to a
horse. I did show it to a second lieutenant in
the horse lines and he said it would count as
Cruelty to Animals. It's currently spread over a
packing case in our quarters as a fetching sort
of tablecloth. The other chaps think it's very
amusing, but I can just see Kitty working away at
it for all that time, so I can't bring myself to get
rid of it. When all this is done and we come home
I suppose I shall have to tell her the horse gave it
back. I did give her mints to some horses pulling
guns up to the line, the poor brutes needed a treat.

I haven't missed Kitty's birthday, have I? Do

write and let me know, as some of the men are very good at making things, and I'm sure I can scrounge up some sort of present.

Love,

David

20 May 1916

Dearest David,

Kitty's birthday is July 15. I can't believe you don't know. Do you know when my birthday is?

You had better eat that stupid crochet, don't you dare bring it home. Kitty is so bumptious about there being a horse in France wearing it, she would never forgive you.

Love,

Evie

PS My birthday was last week. You missed it, but I don't mind much as I expect you were busy.

5 June 1916

Dear Darling Evie,

I'm so sorry I forgot about your birthday. Even though you're right and I was a bit busy. We were under very heavy bombardment for a while, and then our company took part in an attack which was a bit frightening - absolute hail of machine gun fire from Fritz and co. Quite clear that we weren't getting anywhere. Trevors and I dug ourselves into the side of a shell crater and waited to see what happened. We seemed to be there for ever, and then everything went quiet, and I risked popping my head up. No movement anywhere around us at all. We heard shouts from our trench, asking if there was any chance we could get back, and we decided we could, even though poor old Trevors had a dud leg. We were crawling back on our fronts anyway so the leg didn't make as much difference as it might have done. We wormed our way along until we got to the trench, and then I had to roll him over the parapet. He fell on the sergeant though, so at least that broke his fall.

Luckily the attack meant that we were sent

back behind the lines for a while. Also had the pleasure of a really good wash for once. They have turned a disused brewery into a laundry and bathhouse. Vats of hot water – absolute luxury.

I have sent this with a little parcel, a bracelet for each of you. They are made of shell casings, and amazingly enough, all the carving is done with a bent old nail. Hogarth in our company is a bit of an expert, and he is always working on something in the evenings when we're behind the lines. Happy late birthday, and please could you give Kitty hers when the time comes, as we are going back soon, and I think we will be pretty busy.

Much love,

David

4 July 1916

Dear David,

Thank you for the beautiful bracelet, the flower engraving looks far too delicate to have been made with a nail. I have hidden Kitty's,

198

and she is desperate to find out where. I keep discovering her in my bedroom, squirrelling under the mattress. Please, please tell me that you were not hurt crawling back to the trench? You never usually let us know what the fighting is really like, but I'm glad you did this time. Is poor Trevors badly wounded? Has he been sent home? Surely you must be due some leave very soon, it's months since last time.

Please keep safe. The news from the front is so very bad now – did you know about the big push? Is that why you said you thought you would be pretty busy around Kitty's birthday? Mama is terribly frightened about you. I hate to tell you this, but I think she may write to the War Office about your age. There was something in the newspaper about boys who had enlisted too young. The rules have changed now that there is conscription, and she can ask for you to be sent back.

Much love,

Evie

6 July 1916

Dear Sir,

I wish to inform you that my son, David Maitland, currently serving in France as part of the 6th Battalion, King's Own Yorkshire Light Infantry, enlisted under false pretences at Whitby in January 1915. He gave his date of birth as 11 February 1896, stating that at the time of his enlistment, he was eighteen years old, and would shortly be nineteen.

My son was in fact only fifteen years old when he enlisted. His true year of birth was 1899, and at this time he is still only seventeen. I enclose his birth certificate.

I would like to request that my son be returned home to England. He should not be in the army, as he is not eighteen, let alone serving abroad, for which I believe the required age is nineteen.

Yours faithfully,

Helen Maitland

23 October 1916

Mrs Maitland,

In reply to your letter of the 6th July, I know your son David well, as he is assigned to my command. He is an excellent junior officer, much liked by the men, and highly efficient. I am astonished to hear that he is so much under the regulation age. He is very tall and well grown, looking easily into his twenties.

As you will understand, we are hard-pressed here, and I am reluctant to send such a useful officer back home. I do not feel it is necessary to dismiss him as underage when he is so physically big and strong. The rule is, if the boy is up to the work, he should stay, whether he is underage or not.

You will be pleased to hear that your son has been a great credit to you in our engagement with the enemy over the past few weeks.

I am

Yours sincerely

A. L. Keens Lt Col

Commd 6th Battalion K. O. Y. L. I.

Chapter Eleven

"Although I only knew Norman Storrar for a short time, I've been told so many of your reminiscences that I feel as though I knew him quite well. I do wish I'd had the chance to know him better." Miss Boyd looked around at the other staff gathered on the little stage at the front of the assembly hall. "He was, of course, a much loved member of our school, and we know how much he was valued by his comrades and his senior officers. We will be preparing an album for Mr and Mrs Storrar – Miss Douthett has kindly volunteered to take charge – as a keepsake of his time here at the County School. If any of you of have photographs of Norman perhaps in a school team, or a programme from a school concert, we would be very grateful to receive it. Miss Douthett will be asking some of the more talented among you to contribute." Miss Boyd nodded to the music teacher at the piano. "We will conclude with a hymn. Miss Ferrars."

"That'll be you," Grace whispered out of the side of her mouth as she pretended to sing.

"Ssshhh." Evie looked around. "Was he at the school at the same time as you? Do you remember him?"

Grace frowned. "I think he was the school captain when I first came. I was only one of the babies, so I don't honestly remember much. We only really see the boys at assembly, anyway. I shouldn't think I ever spoke to him. But it's still desperately sad, isn't it." She sighed and went back to proper singing, but on the way out of assembly, she whispered, "Our gardener was killed a few days ago, too. His wife came up to the house to tell us. Daddy went off into his study and I think he might even have cried. I know that sounds silly, but they were both terribly keen on dahlias, and Daddy used to win prizes for them at the horticultural show. He always said it was really Arbuthnot who won, and he used to give him a bottle of whisky every time. Mama is going to send all our mending to Mrs Arbuthnot now, even though she could quite easily do it herself; she said Mrs Arbuthnot will need the work."

Evie shivered. "I can't believe everyone thought that the war wouldn't last beyond 1914. It's nearly three years now, and there doesn't seem to be any sign of it stopping."

"Oh, but the Americans," Dot whispered from her other side. "That's sure to make a huge difference, isn't it, them coming in."

"I suppose. It just seems to have been the war for such an awfully long time." Evie sighed, as she slumped down at her desk. "David really is eighteen and old enough to be a soldier now. Mama still hasn't given up hope of him coming home, she still keeps writing letters. I should think the lieutenant colonel has got quite sick of her. Or he would have done if it was the same one." She perked up a little. "Still, he does think he'll have leave soon. It'll be lovely if it's in the summer holidays – we can take the dogs out, and go sketching, and – and everything will be like it was, for a little bit."

There was silence for a second or two, and then Dot said brightly, "We'd better get our books out. French, and then natural history. Miss Lane will be in an awful bate if we're not ready."

"Kitty, stop feeding that dog under the table." Daddy sighed. "Don't tell me you weren't, I can hear him chewing."

"He's hungry, Daddy," Kitty said. "He gives me such pleading looks, I can't not. Besides, it was only my toast crusts."

"Crusts are good for you," Mama murmured.

"They are both awfully hungry," Evie put in, speaking a little louder than usual. There was a small ginger paw tapping at her skirt, and Max was even noisier with toast crusts than Brandy. "Their dinners are so small now, even Max doesn't get enough. Brandy's actually starting to look a bit skinny."

Daddy folded the paper and laid it down by his plate. "Well. It won't be a problem for much longer."

"What do you mean?" Evie dropped the crust she'd been trying to pass subtly to Max, and felt him pounce on it eagerly. "You're not talking about sending Max away again? No one's said anything more about him being a German dog, Daddy, no one."

Her father drummed his fingers on the tablecloth irritably. He still hated to be reminded of the boys on the cliff, and Evie bit her lip, wishing she'd had the sense to stay quiet. She coughed a little, to try and hide the enthusiastic gulping of toast from under the table.

"I'm not talking about Max," Daddy said slowly. "Although he is a little glutton. No. Brandy is going to Essex."

"What? Why?" Evie gasped, and Kitty wailed, "You can't get rid of Brandy!"

"Charles, what are you talking about?" Mama stared at him. "You haven't mentioned this to me."

Daddy reached inside his jacket and pulled out a folded piece of newspaper. "I saw this a few weeks ago – an advertisement in the paper. It's for the War Dog School, in Shoeburyness. Run by a Lieutenant-Colonel Richardson. They use dogs in the German army already, you know, and for the Red Cross. They carry first aid kits to injured men, that sort of thing. This chap is training dogs to be messengers, to carry important signals along the front line. Absolutely vital work."

"In France?" Evie faltered. "You're sending Brandy to France?"

"Well, if he proves suitable." Her father nodded. "I expect he will, though. This Lieutenant Colonel Richardson particularly asked for Airedales. The most suitable breed, apparently. Brave, adaptable, clever. They take very well to training, it says so here. That's what made me think of Brandy."

"You can't," Kitty whimpered. "Please, Daddy, no."

Evie looked over at her, and saw a tawny head appear from under the table. Brandy put his nose in Kitty's lap, looking up at her anxiously. He didn't know what was happening, of course, Evie told herself. It wasn't that he knew he was going to be sent away. He was just worrying about Kitty – he didn't like it when anyone cried. She pressed her hand against her mouth. This was her fault. Hers, and Max's, for getting into trouble with those stupid boys. But Brandy had been the one to save them – without Brandy, the boys might well have thrown Max down the cliff side.

"Kitty," her father said gently. "I know it's hard,

but we have to do our bit. Think of it as Brandy being called up, like a soldier. David has gone to fight, and Brandy must too."

Kitty shook her head, gulping sobs, and then wriggled off her chair and ran out of the dining room, clattering away up the stairs. Brandy stood by the dining room door looking at her go, his tail flicking from side to side in puzzlement. Then he turned back to gaze at Evie with soft, dark eyes, and she stared down at her napkin. She couldn't bear to look at him.

"It isn't going to happen. Daddy wouldn't," Kitty said stubbornly. She had been upstairs crying for ages, and her eyes were still reddened and sore, but she had stamped down the stairs after Daddy had left for the office and coaxed Brandy out into the garden. She was lying on a rug, curled around him, and the big Airedale was stretched out on his back with his legs everywhere. He kept snorting happily to himself as Kitty ran her fingers through his fur. Evie was sitting on his other side, with Max in her lap.

"I know you don't want to believe it," she said slowly. "I don't want to either. But he had the newspaper clipping, Kitty, and he said he'd written to them. He's quite serious."

"No."

"It's because of Max." Evie's voice dropped to a miserable whisper. "It's my fault. Daddy was so angry that those boys said we were unpatriotic. He feels as if he has to make up for it. I'm sure that's why."

Kitty sat up suddenly and glared at her. "You're quite right, it is your fault. So you'd better do something about it, because if Brandy has to go to France I shall never speak to you again. Never, ever, ever!" Then she stumbled up and marched away across the garden to the side door, slamming it behind her.

Evie settled back on the rug, and Brandy came to stand beside her, resting his chin lovingly on her shoulder. "She doesn't really mean it," Evie murmured. She was silent for a moment, and then she added, "Or maybe she does. She probably does, actually, and she's right. I'll have to do something." She looked round at Brandy, and he flicked his ears at her enquiringly. "I don't know either. . ." she whispered.

Nothing more was said about the War Dog School for a few weeks, and Evie began to hope that their father had forgotten. Or perhaps Lieutenant Colonel Richardson had had so many offers of dogs for the school that he hadn't bothered to reply. Then David came home on leave, and since it was the summer holiday, there was such a stream of picnics and swims and sketching expeditions that Evie forgot to worry. Until her father opened a letter at the breakfast table and nodded at it thoughtfully.

"Good. This is from Richardson – the man at the War Dog School. He's asking me to send

Brandy down by train on Thursday, and they'll have someone to meet him at King's Cross."

"No!" Kitty yelped, and then she kicked Evie's ankle. "You said you'd do something," she hissed furiously.

"I didn't," Evie started to say, but her father tucked the letter back into its envelope and glared at them both. "Be quiet. This ridiculous fuss has to stop, both of you. Think of all the families who've given up their sons for the war – I can't believe that you two can be so selfish about a dog. No, Kitty, be silent."

Kitty sat crying into her toast, and Evie pushed her plate away.

"What's happening?" David asked her, once their father had left for the office and Mama had gone to talk to Mrs Dixon about the food shortages and what they could reasonably expect for dinner. Kitty had raced away as soon as she could, probably to howl upstairs, Evie thought guiltily. "Where's Brandy going?"

212

"We wrote to you about it," Evie told him indignantly. "Father's sending him to the War Dog School. It's at Shoeburyness in Essex – they have it there because it's where the Royal Artillery School is, so the dogs get used to hearing the guns all the time." She shuddered.

"Oh. Yes . . . I remember now. But it's a good idea, you know. I've seen messenger dogs carrying messages and situation reports, we're just starting to use them. They're much better than a runner – they can get through mud and shell holes so quickly, broken ground means nothing to them. You know how fast and fit Brandy is. And the keepers adore their dogs, he'll be very well looked after."

"He's very well looked after here," Evie said, staring helplessly at her brother. How could he not understand? He'd spent hours walking and playing with Brandy. He couldn't want this to happen. "He – he's a pet, David. He's *ours*. He won't understand machine guns or shells, or – or gas."

David sighed. "Neither does a boy sent out to France who's never even been to the seaside, Evie. That sort of thing doesn't matter now."

Evie folded up her napkin and jammed it into the ring with short, sharp pushes. It wasn't the same, not at all, she thought to herself as she stalked out into the garden with the dogs trotting after her. People were different, people understood what was happening. Brandy had no idea that he was an English dog, and he ought to fight Germans. It was exactly as stupid as saying that Max was an enemy because dachshunds came from Germany. She had thought her brother would understand, but he was just like Daddy. Both of them seemed to be looking at Brandy as if he were something useful, and they were going to use him up.

Kitty was right, they couldn't let it happen. But there were only two days until Thursday, and Daddy had forbidden them to even mention Brandy going away. It was quite clear that she and Kitty weren't going to be able to talk him round. It wasn't as if Daddy didn't love Brandy, Evie knew that he did, but that didn't seem to matter any more.

What was she going to do?

"I'm not letting you go," she whispered, stroking Brandy's flopped-over ears. "They can't do it, it's wrong." She wandered round the edge of the vegetable patch and pulled up a few weeds between the carrot seedlings. Then she stopped, looking thoughtfully at Brandy. "Daddy can't send you to Shoeburyness if you're not here."

Brandy waved his stubby tail in a friendly manner, since he could tell she was talking to him, and Max barked shrilly at a sparrow that had dared to land among the winter cabbages. "Don't chase it!" Evie grabbed him with a practised hand. "And ssshhh. I'm thinking."

At first she wondered if Grace would hide Brandy for her, or maybe even Elaine, since she already had Jet and obviously liked dogs. But somehow it was hard to imagine explaining to either of them that she didn't want him to go to France. Not even to Grace, who was her best friend. In fact especially not to Grace, as her brother was out there fighting. She was almost sure that Grace would think a dog was a lot less important than a brother.

Evie pushed that thought away hurriedly. It was no good relying on anyone else. Not even Kitty, since she was useless at secrets. They made her go pink, and giggle, and stuff her hands into her mouth as if she needed to stop the words falling out.

She needed somewhere to take Brandy until after tomorrow – maybe even for longer. Until Daddy had given up and told the lieutenant colonel that he wouldn't be sending his Airedale after all. When Brandy came back then, Evie was pretty sure it would be too embarrassing to write again.

"Evie?" Mama swept into the nursery, and Evie looked up in pretend surprise. She *was* actually a little bit surprised, as she had been expecting Daddy. "Darling, do you know where Brandy is?"

Evie restrained herself from looking around the room, as if she expected to find Brandy behind one of the creaky basketwork armchairs. She mustn't overact. "I haven't seen him for ages," she said thoughtfully. "Not since just after breakfast." And that was actually true.

"Are you sure?" Mama stared at her searchingly. "Sarah says he hasn't come for his dinner, and that's very unusual. Daddy is – worried."

"Oh! Well, I'm worried too." Evie stood up, carefully catching Max, who was asleep between her and the side of the chair. He was a very thorough sleeper, and she didn't want him to fall off. "Daddy hasn't seen him then?"

"No . . . and after this morning. . ." Mama sighed. "You'd better come downstairs and talk to him."

Evie followed her, and saw that Kitty was peering round the door of her bedroom, and then following too.

Downstairs, their father was standing by the front door, calling out into the garden. He swung round as Mama and the girls came down, and eyed them both sternly. "Do either of you know where Brandy is? He's disappeared, which is frankly suspicious, bearing in mind my letter this morning."

Kitty shook her head. "I don't know. Maybe he ran away because he didn't want to go to France?"

"Don't be ridiculous, Kitty," her father snapped. "Evie?"

"I don't know either," Evie said, trying to make her voice sound normal. But it was difficult when she couldn't remember what her voice was supposed to sound like. She had a horrible feeling that absolutely everyone knew she was lying, and her cheeks were getting hot.

David clanged the front gate shut and walked up the garden. "I've been down the street calling," he said as he came up the steps. "No sign of him. He doesn't usually go wandering, does he?"

"Never," her father said, staring pointedly at Evie.

"I honestly haven't seen him since just after breakfast," Evie repeated. "He must have got out of the garden somehow. Perhaps when Mrs Elders brought the post?"

"No, he likes Mrs Elders, he always walks with her to the door if he's outside," Mama murmured. "Evie, I can't help thinking you must know something about this. You usually walk the dogs in the morning when you're at home."

"Of course she knows about it! She knows exactly where he is. You'd better go to your room and think, Evie. When you've come to your senses and you're ready to tell me what you've done with him, you can come downstairs."

"But, Daddy, I was about to take Max for a walk! And Brandy, I didn't even know he wasn't here," Evie added quickly.

"Just let him out in the garden. Or David can take the dratted creature out."

"Really?" David sighed, and eyed Max with reluctance. He didn't mind playing with him in the garden, but walking him, in uniform – it wasn't very dignified.

"David doesn't want to – you know he feels silly walking Max because he's so little," Evie said. "I can take him, Daddy. Just quickly. Then I'll go to my room, if you like."

"You're going to your room now," her father said calmly. "You'll stay there, as I said. You won't be able to nip out and feed Brandy, wherever you've put him. He'll have to go hungry. You can think about that."

Kitty turned wide-eyed to stare at Evie. "You've hidden him?"

"No, I haven't!" Evie snapped. "I don't know where he is!" Except that of course she had, and she did, and she knew that he'd be curled up on the old blanket she'd left, confused and wanting his supper. What was she going to do now? Even if Daddy did let her take Max out for a quick walk, someone would be watching. She hadn't managed to sneak any scraps for Brandy yet, and she wouldn't be able to get out and feed him, not without Daddy or David realizing how long she'd been gone. When she'd been trying to think of hiding places, she'd remembered an abandoned shed on the path along the East Cliff, and it had seemed a good idea for Brandy to be hidden so far away. But it meant going all through the town and up the Church Steps, and then along the cliff path. It was almost as far as the tea hut, the one the ambulance men had used for the injured from the shipwreck, but Evie hadn't been able to think of anywhere else.

Perhaps she could tell Kitty, she wondered, eyeing her little sister cautiously. Maybe she'd be able to keep a secret, just this once? She was desperate for Brandy not to be sent away. She could slip out and take Brandy something to eat.

"Thank you," Kitty whispered, sneaking her hand into Evie's.

"Leave her alone, Kitty. Evie, go upstairs. The two of you aren't to talk to each other. And Kitty, stop looking at your sister as if she's done something clever, this is just pointless disobedience – and dishonesty. You should be ashamed to behave like this. To lie to me."

Evie stared back at him. "I haven't seen Brandy since just after breakfast," she said again, but she could hear her voice shaking. Her father looked so angry – white-faced and furious, like he had after the boys had threatened her and Max. At least then it hadn't really been her that he'd been angry with. She'd never defied her parents like this before, and it was making her feel sick.

If it hadn't been for Daddy wanting to get rid of Max the summer before last, she thought as she stumbled up the stairs, she might have given in and told him. But he had been wrong then, and he was wrong now, she was sure. She kept thinking of Brandy, all alone and hungry in that old shed on the cliff. It was quite true that he wouldn't understand being sent away to the war – but he wouldn't understand why Evie had tied him up and left him, either.

Evie woke to a scratching on her bedroom door, and sat up, blinking and confused. It was almost dark – she had cried herself to sleep, she realized, pressing her hand against her swollen eyes. David must have taken Max out, and now he was back, and wanting her. Was she allowed to open her door and let him in? No one had said...

She crept across the bedroom and turned the door handle cautiously. Max was there, his tail flailing excitedly. Evie hardly noticed as he bounced into the room and circled about, happily sniffing. Behind him, looking at her enquiringly, as if he wasn't quite sure of his welcome, was Brandy. He wagged his stub of a tail at her, and he had that same puzzled look in his dark eyes, the look he'd had when she looked round the door of the shed, just before she'd closed it.

"Oh, Brandy." Evie crouched down and stroked his ears. "Did you chew through that rope? I suppose it was awfully old. Why couldn't you have stayed?"

The Airedale flattened his ears guiltily. She had told him to stay, and he hadn't.

"He didn't chew the rope."

Evie looked up in surprise. She hadn't noticed David standing at the top of the stairs. "Well, he must have done. I tied him up."

"Mmm. I undid him."

Evie got up, slowly. Her knees were shaking. "You found him, you mean? How?" She shook her head, not understanding. "Did you follow me this morning? Why would you?"

David sighed. "I took Max out, didn't I? He knew where Brandy was. He wanted to go and find him, Evie. I just – let him take me there."

"And then you found him and you untied him and you brought him back?" Evie wailed. "Why? Don't you understand? Daddy's going to put him on a train tomorrow!"

"I know that," her brother said patiently. "What I don't understand is why you're being like this about it, Evie! All the knitting you've done, and the fundraising with the girls from school – you're always at it. First aid classes, and bandage rolling, and Mama says you're even wanting to go and volunteer at the hospital. I don't see how you can be working so hard for the war effort and not want Brandy to do his bit. He'll be useful, Evie, probably more useful than I am out there."

"I told you!" Evie's voice rose. "You're out there because you chose to be! You really did, you lied about your age and made all that fuss to get there. And even the boys who are going now, the ones who have to go, at least they know what the war *is*."

David stared at her, and then he laughed, and suddenly Evie noticed how thin he was, because of the shadows on his face when he laughed like that, with his mouth open. He sat down on the top step of the stairs, like a little boy, except for his uniform. Brandy stood looking down at him uneasily, and Max stood behind Evie, instead of throwing himself into David's lap, the way he usually did when anyone sat on the floor.

"It isn't funny!"

"No, it bloody isn't." He shook his head. "Do you actually think any of us knew what it would be like? Evie, do you?" He reached out and grabbed hold of her wrist, dragging her closer.

She shook her head, frightened by the look in his eyes, and tried to pull away. He didn't let go. "Do you know, the trench we were in just before I came on leave had bones sticking out of the side of it? Skulls, Evie. Bits of men. The fighting was so heavy there a year or so ago that they didn't have time to bury the bodies properly, they just dug holes in the sides of the trenches, and of course they're all collapsing with the rain. They smell. Did you know that?"

"No," Evie whispered. She had stopped trying to pull now, and just looked at him.

"The earth shakes because of the guns, and

there are great shrieking shells flying over us half the time. Almost all the men I trained with are dead, did I tell you?"

Evie shook her head.

"No one knows what it's like, Evie." He pulled her closer and hissed into her face. "No one." Then he dropped her wrist, and leaned back against the banisters with his eyes closed.

Evie scrambled over his feet and ran down the stairs, the dogs pattering after her. She banged the side door open and raced out into the garden, stumbling about in the half-dark, and at last throwing herself down on the stone bench under the chestnut tree by the wall. In the daytime, greenish sunlight filtered down through the leaves, and it was Brandy's favourite place to lie.

David had never spoken to her like that before. He'd never looked at her like that, as if he hated her. Shivering, she sat up and pulled the metal bracelet he had sent her off her wrist. She wore it so often that there was a faint greyish mark on her skin, where it had rubbed. She scrabbled at the grass growing around the bench – long and untrimmed now that Jack had gone – and scraped a hole, burying the bracelet. She rubbed angrily at the mark, wishing she could bury that too, but it wouldn't go.

Evie had expected that her father would keep on being coldly furious – that he'd send her back to her room, because she'd tried to hide Brandy, and then lied about it, but he didn't. Instead, he was the one who came to find her when she missed dinner that night, following a wavering lantern light through the dark garden. He didn't say anything about what she'd done, just took her to the kitchen, and got Mrs Dixon to give her bread and jam, and then told her to go to bed.

"What happened?" Kitty whispered, sitting on Evie's bed the next morning. "David came down to dinner looking like a ghost and didn't eat anything. It was horrible. And then Sarah came in with the rice pudding and said that she'd taken you up some and you weren't in your room. Mama said you'd probably run away with Brandy this time, and she told Daddy he was heartless."

"I don't want to talk about it," Evie muttered. "I was only in the garden." Not for anything would she tell Kitty what David had said. She couldn't bear to. At least there were only a couple more days of his leave.

She sighed. "So, are you talking to me? Even though Brandy still has to go?"

Kitty swallowed hard. "Daddy's downstairs brushing him. So he looks his best when he gets there. At least you tried."

"I don't even think he'll be a very good messenger," Evie burst out. "He's not used to leaping over mud, and I expect he'll be terrified of the guns." But that made her think of David, yesterday, and she shivered convulsively.

"Oh, don't," Kitty said, her voice husky, and she leaned over to give Evie a hug. "He'll be fabulous. Maybe he'll get a medal," she sniffed. "Or be mentioned in dispatches. That'll be one in the eye for David, he never has been. I can't think how he was so stupid – even if Max did show him where Brandy was, he didn't have to bring him back."

"What time's the train?" Evie asked.

"Eleven-ish. Daddy says we can go to the station with him, if we promise faithfully to behave." Kitty rested her chin on her knees. "I think that means we aren't allowed to howl, and I'm not sure I can. Not howl, I mean."

"Me neither." Evie picked up Max, who was lying in a saggy heap at the edge of the bed. He hung out of her hands like a bean bag, and snuffled awake. "But I think we should go."

Brandy had been in a train before – when they had gone on holiday to Scotland, and visiting their grandmother in London. He seemed to remember the station, and Evie was sure that he was enjoying being out without Max. He sniffed and sneezed when the train came in and the smoke billowed about, but the huge, wheezing train didn't seem to scare him.

Kitty crouched down next to him and started fussing with his collar while he wriggled and tried to lick her face. "Ssshhh," she murmured. "You'll have to get used to it. They'll be tying all sorts of things on to you, I expect."

"Kitty, what are you doing?" their father asked. "We need to take him to the guard's van."

"There. I've done it." Kitty kissed Brandy's nose and stood up. "It's a note, for the school, with another note inside it for the soldier who takes care of him when he goes to France. Telling them that they'd better look after him, and how he likes to have gravy with his dinner. And giving them our address, so that they can write and tell us when he does something terribly brave."

Daddy only nodded, instead of telling Kitty that Brandy was going to be a soldier now, and would just have to eat what everyone else ate, and he didn't say she had to take the note off. All he said was, "It's down at the end of the train."

Brandy looked puzzled when his lead was

handed over and Evie and Kitty and their father didn't follow him up the steps into the guard's van, but it was only when the door was closed, and the train began to hiss and clank, that he realized they weren't coming with him. There was a scuffling sound, only just audible above the noise of the train, and then a dreadful, high-pitched, frantic howling.

"Brandy, oh no. . ." Evie heard herself say, and she started to run along the platform after the train. It was going so slowly, they could probably catch the door handle and let him out. No one could make him go, not when he was crying like that. Even Daddy would see. . .

But the train was gathering speed, surging out of the station like Brandy himself racing along the beach. Faster and louder, so that she and Kitty could only just hear those desperate noises as they came to the end of the platform, and there was nowhere left to run, and the train pulled away with Brandy in it.

Chapter Twelve

"Goodbye, then."

Evie nodded, and leaned forward to embrace David – not throwing her arms around him as she would always have done before, not burying her face in the scratchy wool of his uniform, but kissing him politely on the cheek and patting his arm. It was perfectly reasonable – she was fourteen now, after all. She shouldn't be childish and emotional. Kitty didn't hug him either, though.

Evie had avoided her brother for the last two days of his leave, meeting him politely at meals, but pleading tiredness when he suggested a walk along the cliffs, or a sketching trip to the abbey.

Walks were horrible anyway. She and Kitty missed Brandy, but in all their horror and panic over his leaving, they hadn't thought of Max. The little dog didn't understand what had happened. Evie had never thought that he and Brandy liked each other that much – Brandy endured Max, and Max adored waltzing in front of the older dog to make sure he got the fuss and treats he knew he deserved. But now he was bereft. He had greeted Kitty and Evie on their return from the station with puzzled tail-wagging. He stood there at the open front door, clearly looking down the garden and waiting for Brandy to appear. They had taken Brandy out and left him behind, which wasn't that unusual, since he was known to sit down and sulk on longer walks. But now they were back. So where had Brandy gone?

Evie had just about managed to stop crying by the time they'd walked back from the station – their father had come prepared with two large handkerchiefs, but had been clearly horrified by the state they were in, and had escaped to his office as soon as it was decently possible. She'd had to recover enough to lead Kitty, blind with tears, back to the house. Then Max's confused eyes and doubtfully wagging tail had set her off all over again. She had picked him up and pushed Kitty up the stairs to the nursery, where all three of them curled together to cry in one rickety armchair, and nearly collapsed it altogether.

The next morning Evie had only planned a very short walk, perhaps along St Hilda's Terrace and then back down – Max wouldn't mind, and all their favourite walks would only make her think of poor Brandy, who must be shut up in a kennel at the War Dog School by now. Max had other ideas. He refused to turn right out of the gate, actually sitting down and squealing when she gently tried to pull. He marched, as determinedly as only a dachshund can march, down the hill and through the middle of Whitby to the bridge, and the road up past the church to the cliffs.

As they reached the hundred and ninety-nine steps, Evie suddenly realized what he was doing, and stopped, just as Max was preparing himself for the effort.

"No. Oh, Max darling, no." She crouched down to look at him, not caring that her skirt was trailing in the dust, that she was becoming a young lady now, and must always be polite and tidy in public. She ran her hand over the thin velvet fur of his domed head, and gently tugged one silken ear. "He isn't there. I know he was before, but this is different. Oh, Max, he isn't coming back."

Kitty had gone to sleep at last the night before assuring her that the war would be over soon — everyone knew that the Germans would never last, now that America had come into the war and was drafting men like anything. The last thing she'd said was, "And then they'll send him back, won't they?"

Evie had nodded, and whispered huskily, "Of course." But she didn't think they would. The dogs were out there to take the risks that the men couldn't, or wouldn't. They had to run along the front line to take back priceless messages, the frantic demands for more men. The dogs could only do it because they didn't understand the danger they were in. They didn't, did they? She could only keep on hoping not, that Brandy would think it was all one long exciting game – until it ended.

Max looked up at the steps, stretching above him, the steps he always insisted that he be carried up, and then he looked back at Evie. He put one small ginger paw on the lowest step and set off, dragging himself grimly up the Church Stairs for the first time ever. He refused to be turned back, and when Evie picked him up, he struggled and flailed and thumped his head on the underside of her chin and she had to put him down again. And then he went on clambering sturdily up the steps, and on through the churchyard to the cliff path.

When they reached the empty stone shed, he clawed at the door until she unlatched it and let him go in. He sniffed his way eagerly around, as though he couldn't just *see* that Brandy wasn't there. When he'd tracked back and forth across the whole, tiny, cobwebbed place, he sat down in the middle of the floor and howled, almost as loud as Brandy had the day before.

Since then, Evie hadn't taken him out of the garden.

Mama and Daddy were walking down to the station to see David off, but Kitty had started to cry at breakfast just at the thought of it, so she and Evie were staying behind.

"I'm sorry, Evie," David murmured. "I didn't mean to – to upset you, the other night."

"I know." She tried to smile at him, but it didn't come out very well. "Goodbye – and – and good luck." She tried another hug, a little better this time but still stiff, and then found that she wanted to cry again as he went down the steps and turned back to wave.

"Do you know," Kitty muttered beside her, "I'm almost looking forward to going back to school."

"There's a telegram, Mama." Kitty sidled slowly into the parlour, holding the yellow envelope out in front of her. Now that Sarah was the only maid they had, Evie and Kitty would answer the door if they were home, to save her running up from the kitchen. Kitty loved opening the front door to callers, but now she was obviously wishing she hadn't dashed along the hallway to get there first. Telegrams these days meant news, the worst kind of news.

The girls' mother got up from the table where she'd been writing letters, dropping her pen and leaving a trail of little ink spots across her page. Kitty held the envelope out to her, but Mama didn't take it. She rubbed her hands down the skirts of her dress, as though she wasn't quite sure what to do with them.

"Aren't you going to open it?" Kitty asked, her voice squeaky with fright.

"I— Yes. I suppose." Mama took the envelope, and tore the flap open, very carefully, a bit at a time. As though it mattered! Evie wanted to scream at her to hurry up.

"Is he injured?" she asked urgently. "Or ... missing?"

Mama shook her head, and held out the fragile piece of paper.

Deeply regret to inform you your son 2nd Lt D R Maitland was killed on active service 25th August letter follows the Army Council express their sympathy

All Evie could think was, *I should have hugged him properly.*

The letter that came a few days later was quite short, and didn't tell them very much, except that his commanding officer was so sorry, and David had been a very brave and competent officer. There were no details – nothing about what exactly had happened, or where he had been buried. The girls' mother kept on reading it, repeating the words to herself in different voices, as if it would change what they meant.

Evie and Kitty went to school in black armbands, just as they had for Alecky when they first started there three years before. This time, though, they weren't the only ones. So many of them had lost a brother, or a father, or an uncle.

"How is your mother?" Grace asked delicately as she and Evie and Sybil sat out on the grass after lunch.

Evie sighed. "I suppose not as bad as I thought she would be. My father seems more upset than she does, he's so silent. But . . . Mama thought David would be protected by angels. She kept a card with a painting of them next to his photograph in her room. And now. . ." She glanced worriedly at her two friends. "Now she thinks the angels have taken

241

him, which I do too, in a way, I mean, I'm sure he's in heaven. It's just that Mama thinks she's going to talk to him."

"What?" Grace, who'd been twisting her fingers together anxiously, the way she did when she was worrying about Harold, sat up and stared at Evie.

"It's one of the ladies at church. Mrs Weatherill, do you know her? She always sings very loudly in the hymns, and she makes faces."

Grace snorted. "Oh, yes, her. She cries in the prayers as well."

"Mmmm. She's going to introduce Mama to a spiritualist."

"A real one?" Sybil asked, wide-eyed. "You mean a medium? Who talks to ghosts and has ectoplasm and things?"

"I don't know about ectoplasm," Evie admitted. "Is it something they do?"

Sybil nodded. "Marjorie went to a séance in London, she told me about it. It was awfully dramatic. The medium was absolutely covered in ectoplasm."

"But what is it?" Grace asked.

"A sort of jelly, I think," Sybil said doubtfully. "But with faces on, or sometimes it looks like a person. A spirit, I mean."

"Do you believe in spirits?" Evie looked between them. "Ones that can come back and talk? It's just that I'm not sure I do, and I know Daddy says it's nonsense, but Mama really believes. She was so grateful to Mrs Weatherill, and she keeps talking about it. She and Daddy, well, they argued..." She sighed miserably. "He said she mustn't have Eugenia – that's the spiritualist – in the house, but she's going to anyway. And she says Kitty and I have to be there too, because we need as many people that David loved in the room as possible, to call him back."

Grace shifted closer, and put an arm around her. "Don't you want to?"

"I don't know!" Evie sniffed. "On his last leave, I was so angry with him. Because he—" She faltered. She didn't want to tell Grace the awful things that David had said about the bones in the trench, and how frightened he was. How would it make her friend feel, with Harold still out there? "I hid Brandy," she admitted, since she had to say something. "Daddy wanted to send him to train as a messenger dog for the soldiers in France, and I couldn't bear it, so I hid him. Then David went and found him and brought him back, and it was all for nothing."

"Brandy's gone?" Grace said, shocked.

"He's at a school in Essex being trained. I miss him so much." She looked apologetically at Grace. "Almost more than I miss David. He was away at school, you see, and he was so busy in the holidays, and then he went off to be a soldier, but Brandy was always there, and you couldn't help loving him. I blamed David. I was still angry when he went back, and I didn't say goodbye properly, and now I wish I had."

Grace nodded. "So if this spiritualist *is* real, you actually could."

"But it seems so odd. . . I mean, Mrs Weatherill told Mama that Eugenia would speak in David's voice." Evie shivered, and felt Grace's arm tighten around her.

"Marjorie said the lady she saw knew things that no one could possibly have known – but she wouldn't tell me what," Sybil put in. "She thought it was all nonsense before she went though. When are you seeing this Eugenia?"

"She's coming to the house tomorrow evening. Mama had to wait until my father would be out, and he has a night shift tomorrow." She leaned forward, sinking her chin in her hands, and muttered, "I wish I just *knew.*"

"It isn't right, Miss Evie," Mrs Dixon said, thumping at the bread dough to show how much she disapproved.

"Bad enough getting mixed up with such stuff, but goin' behind Mr Maitland's back." Sarah shook her head.

"She only wants to talk to him," Evie murmured. "You know how much she misses him. I think she's hoping that he's with Alecky, and they're looking after each other."

Sarah sighed. "Poor dear."

"Both of her boys." Mrs Dixon rubbed at her nose with a floury hand. "It seems cruel hard. Yes, go on then, I'll send up tea and a plate of parkin or somesuch, and she'll have to be happy with that. I can't be making shortbread or fancies, not with t'age Sarah had to queue at t'grocer's this morning, and bringing home next to nothing."

"Thank you, Mrs Dixon." Evie hurried back upstairs, trying to remember what else was on the list of tasks Mama had given her. She decided not to worry about changing her petticoat, since it really was quite clean already. Mama had said that it was important for them all to be clean from the skin out so as to make sure the spirits felt welcome. But Mama hadn't heard Sarah complaining about the ironing, and Evie was fairly sure that David wouldn't notice anyway. She rubbed the dusty toes of her shoes down the back of the other stocking leg, just in case.

"Hurry up." Kitty appeared at the top of the back stairs in her sailor dress, her hair strained tightly into fresh bows. "Mama sent me to fetch you – she says they'll be here any minute. And where's Max, because she says you have to shut him up here so he doesn't disturb the séance."

"He's asleep in the kitchen." Evie had just seen him, curled up on the rag rug by Mrs Dixon's chair. There were more scraps spare for Max now that Brandy was gone, and he'd been wandering around the house looking so lost that Mrs Dixon and Sarah had started to make more fuss of him.

Kitty clutched suddenly at Evie's hand as the front door bell rang. "It's them!"

Evie patted at her hair, wishing she'd had time to go and brush it out, and then led Kitty along the hallway to let Mrs Weatherill and the medium in.

Mrs Weatherill kissed her enthusiastically, and

patted Kitty, and then turned to usher in a small, neatly dressed woman, who she introduced as Miss Abelard. "Eugenia, you know. Ah, there you are, Helen!"

Mama had come to the door of the parlour. "We're so very glad you're here," she said eagerly to Eugenia. "I do hope you'll be able to help us – Alice has spoken of you so warmly, I'm sure you must be very talented."

"She doesn't look like I thought she would," Kitty whispered, as she and Evie followed them into the parlour. "She hasn't got a turban on, or mystical jewellery, or anything."

"Mystical jewellery?" Evie hissed back. "What were you expecting, half a dead crocodile round her neck? Ssshhh. Mama said we mustn't disturb the vibrations."

"The spirits are fragile," Eugenia was explaining, as the two girls came in. "This is a very beautiful room, of course. I can tell that you have a sympathetic soul, Mrs Maitland, the atmosphere is so quiet and restful. But bright light is too much for our poor brothers and sisters. Perhaps we could draw the curtains, and have just a lamp burning low?"

"Oh, of course." Mama nodded. "Evie, could you. . . ?"

Evie went to unhook the curtain sashes and draw the thick green brocade curtains. It had been a warm day and the sun wouldn't set for another hour, but as she pulled the curtains across, the room gradually sank into a shadowy dimness. So much so that she nearly fell over a small footstool on her way back to stand by her mother. It struck her that it was going to be quite hard to see any ectoplasm.

"So – so what do we do?" Mama asked nervously as she lit a gas lamp and turned it down very low. "I haven't ever tried to communicate with spirits before, though of course we've all heard things. . ."

"Please do not worry, Mrs Maitland," Eugenia said softly. She wasn't quite as young as Evie had first thought; there were wrinkles at the corners of her rather staring blue eyes, and the hand she laid on Mama's sleeve was bony. "Fear is destructive. You must be calm, and have faith."

"Yes . . . of course."

Evie pressed her nails into her palms. She hated to see Mama like this, so eager and anxious. Her mother wanted this to be real so much. Eugenia could do almost anything, Evie thought sadly, and Mama would believe. The medium's soft, whispery voice started to sound more like a hiss.

"Is there a small table? . . . Ah, here." Eugenia pointed to a little tea table close to the fireplace, and Evie and Kitty got up to fetch it.

"Tea, ma'am." The door creaked open, and Sarah edged round it with a tray, peering through the gloom.

"Oh! Shall we have tea?" Mama looked worried. "Would you like any? I know a séance must be exhausting for you, but I don't want to disturb the vibrations."

250

"Perhaps afterwards," Eugenia said sweetly. "I feel the presence of the spirits so very close. We should not delay."

"My goodness, no. Thank you, Sarah, I will ring for tea later."

Sarah, still standing with the heavy tray, sucked in her breath, and then she turned and went out with as much of a flounce as she could manage without dropping the teapot. Mrs Weatherill looked mildly disappointed to miss out on tea, but recovered in the fuss of arranging chairs and making sure that Eugenia was comfortable.

"Now we join hands," the medium explained, reaching out to Mama, and to Mrs Weatherill on her other side.

"Yes." Mama was silent for a moment, waiting. Then she added, "And – and what should we expect? With Evie here, and especially Kitty, they're so young, you see. I don't want them to be frightened."

"No one should be frightened of the spirit

world, Helen," Mrs Weatherill said earnestly. "Our enlightenment is a gift, a true gift sent to us from beyond the veil."

Kitty looked sideways at Evie, and then rolled her eyes, and Evie bit her bottom lip to stop herself giggling. She wanted Eugenia to be a real medium, just so David could know how sorry she was that she'd been angry. She was willing to believe – but no one could make her believe that Mrs Weatherill wasn't an idiot.

"Mrs Weatherill is right," Eugenia said. "We should not fear whatever manifestations the spirits send us. Take hands, girls." She was looking directly at Evie and Kitty, and Evie realized that she had probably seen Kitty roll her eyes. *But she must be used to people doubting her*, Evie thought, ducking her head. Quickly, she grabbed Kitty's hand and Mama's, and muttered, "Hold her hand" to Kitty, who was watching Eugenia curiously and hadn't noticed Mrs Weatherill flapping at her.

"Close your eyes," Eugenia murmured. "While we wait for the loved ones to appear, it will help you to focus. Please do not be afraid if I move, or writhe, or seem to be in pain – I may have to hold back malignant spirits."

Holding hands in a circle, in silence, there *was* a strangeness in the room. Evie could feel it, like a tingling in the air around her. *Not so very different to waiting for a French vocab test to start*, she thought idly, and then frowned at herself. If they didn't take it seriously, there was no chance of them calling a spirit. Mama needed this, and she wanted it to work too, even though it was eerie. She squeezed her eyes tight and tried to think spiritual thoughts.

Kitty's stomach rumbled, and Mrs Weatherill sighed, and then a voice spoke into the waiting.

"I am here."

It wasn't David's voice, not exactly, but it certainly wasn't Eugenia's voice either. Evie felt Kitty and Mama's hands squeeze hers, and all the air in the room seemed to grow thin. She was panting.

"David?" Mama whispered hopefully.

"Yes. Hello, Mama."

"Where are you?"

"In a waiting place."

"Are you – are you well? Not in any pain?" Mama's voice was shaking, and Evie longed to hold her – but that would mean breaking the circle.

"I am beyond physical pain, only so sad to leave you all."

Evie opened her eyes, just a little, to look at Eugenia. After all, if there was going to be ectoplasm and manifestations it would be a pity to miss it. It was hard to see in the dim light, but the medium was still there opposite her, holding Mama and Mrs Weatherill's hands. She was limp in her chair, her head thrown back.

"Oh, my darling," Mama gasped. "We're so sad too. We miss you dreadfully."

"I'm sending all my love, always."

Mama launched into a stumbling explanation of

why their father wasn't with them, begging David to send him some kind of message.

"It doesn't sound like David," Kitty breathed into Evie's ear.

"I know, but he's dead, it probably makes a difference."

"But he didn't talk like that – he sounds like Mrs Weatherill, or the vicar – mystical, you know. And he never said Mama, he called her Mother."

That was true, actually. Evie peered closer at Eugenia, and then squeezed Kitty's hand. "Look! She's glowing!"

Kitty caught her breath. "I – I don't want to. . . Oh. . . I'm going to look. Gosh."

"She is, isn't she?"

Eugenia's face was hard to see as she'd thrown her head back, but there was a faint greenish-white light shining around her neck and head, as though light was seeping out of her skin.

"Ssshhh!" Mrs Weatherill shook Kitty's hand. "You'll disturb the spirits."

"But she's glowing," Kitty whispered back.

"Of course she is." Mrs Weatherill sounded proud. "Eugenia is such a strong medium. The spirits are speaking through her, they're using her energy to communicate with us."

"I must go," Eugenia said loudly, breaking into Mama's tearful pleas for David to find Alecky and bring him to talk to her too. "Other spirits are coming."

"No, don't go!" Mama cried. "Which other spirits – oh, is it Alecky?"

But Eugenia didn't answer. Instead she began to rock backwards and forwards in her chair, groaning and giving strange little wails.

"What's happening? Are they hurting her?" Mama turned worriedly to Mrs Weatherill. "Alice, should we wake her?"

"Not on any account!" Mrs Weatherill said firmly. "Keep hold of her hands. We must link her to the earthly realm, and send her our love and energy. This is such a powerful manifestation,

Helen! We're so lucky to be here, who knows what we'll see?"

"Ectoplasm?" Kitty whispered, sounding half hopeful, half scared. Evie had told her what Sybil had said about it being like jelly.

"Eugenia, speak to us with your spirit voice!" Mrs Weatherill commanded, as Eugenia writhed and whimpered, but the medium stayed silent.

Suddenly, Evie felt Kitty jerk backwards. "Ugh, there's something on the edge of the table!"

"A disembodied hand!" Mrs Weatherill sounded absolutely delighted. "Oh, Helen, do look! I've read about this, but I've never seen it. Eugenia must be so deeply entranced to manifest a spirit hand."

Evie pulled Kitty's hand towards her, squeezing it tight. "If it comes any closer, we'll run away," she whispered. The hand lay limp on the edge of the table, dark fingers splayed. It was horribly eerie, and it seemed to be coming from Eugenia's stomach. The medium was still moaning and twisting in her chair.

"It's Eugenia's own hand," Evie said. "It has to be."

"It isn't, I'm holding her hand," Mama said. "And so is Alice."

"Evie, you must have faith," Mrs Weatherill said. "Don't listen, Eugenia. We must banish these negative energies from around her, girls!"

"But whose hand is it?" Mama asked. "Kitty, don't be afraid, it won't harm you."

"I don't like it," Kitty said miserably, trying to pull her fingers out of Evie's.

"Don't break the circle!" cried Mrs Weatherill. "It's probably you that's calling the spirits, Kitty, children are so strong psychically."

"I'm not, I'm not!" Kitty wailed. "Let me go, I don't like it!"

"Mama, it's scaring her, please can't we stop?" Evie begged. She let go of Kitty's hand and put her arm around her little sister instead.

"But if it's a message from David . . . or Alecky. . ." Mama whispered. "Oh, what should we do?"

Then, with a little snap and a gulp, the spirit hand disappeared, and Eugenia shrieked – a very different noise from the faint wails she'd been uttering up until now.

"What is it?" Mama cried as Eugenia sprang up, pushing away something solid and gibbering in panic. Mrs Weatherill's chair fell over as she jumped back, and Kitty whimpered, "Oh, what is it, what is it? Is it ectoplasm?"

"No, it's Max." Evie ran around the table and grabbed him. "Max, leave! Drop it, you naughty dog! Ugh, what is that?"

Max wriggled out of her arms and darted away, but it was just too dark to chase him. Evie looked round anxiously. She was fairly sure that the séance was over, they must have destroyed the vibrations, so it couldn't matter now if there was more light. She turned up the gas lamp, and then dashed after Max. The dachshund had doubled back out of her way, and now he was under the table, greedily tearing at something between his paws.

"Let go of it!" Evie said, yanking it firmly off him and standing up. "Oh dear."

It was the spirit hand, now even limper, and rather mangled. Max whined crossly, and stood up on his hind paws, scrabbling at Evie's skirt. He wanted it back.

"What has that horrible little creature done?" Mrs Weatherill cried. "Oh, how could you let him, Evie? The damage to Eugenia! You could have killed her!"

"I didn't *let* him do anything," Evie protested. "I think Sarah must have left the door open a crack when you sent her away with the tea, Mama. Max was asleep in the kitchen, but he came up here to see what we were doing."

Mama sat in her chair, her hand pressed to her chest, breathing fast. "I don't understand. What has he done?"

"Um." Evie poked at the remains. "He's eaten the spirit hand."

"But – but isn't it made of ectoplasm?" Kitty

asked, looking at it disgustedly. "It's a spirit thing, how could he eat something from the other side?"

"Give that back to me," Eugenia said furiously, reaching for the reddish lumps, but Evie pulled it away.

"No. I think Mama should see what it is." She stepped back quickly as Eugenia tried to grab for it. "Look, Mama."

"I don't understand." Mama shook her head. "Evie, that looks like liver."

"I don't intend to stay here to be insulted," Eugenia said sharply. "This house is unwelcoming to the spirit world. I can feel the anger and negative emotion pressing on me. I need to leave."

"Of course you do," Mrs Weatherill said soothingly. "I'm so sorry, Eugenia, I should never have brought you here. Helen, you must speak to your girls! How could they behave so badly?"

"We didn't!" Evie said, suddenly furious. "We weren't the ones behaving badly! She's a cheat, can't you see? She was pretending the whole time!

That spirit hand was made of liver, she must have had it up her sleeve, or in a pocket in her skirt."

"That's *disgusting*," Kitty said. "I hate liver."

"And she's still glowing," Evie added. "Because there's streaks of paint on her face. Luminous paint."

"How dare you say such awful things?" Mrs Weatherill wheeled round and marched out of the room, leading Eugenia after her and murmuring, "Don't listen, don't listen, my dear. Helen, I will not be attending your coffee morning in aid of the hospital, some things are just too much to ask."

"None of it was real?" Mama watched them go, and then reached out to Evie pleadingly. "Not – not David either?"

Evie dropped the chewed lump of liver on the table, and came to hold her mother. "I think it was all made up, Mama. I'm so sorry."

"We didn't talk to him?" Kitty asked. "It did *feel* real. I was shivering all over."

"I think it was only Eugenia using a different

voice." Evie sighed. "You were right, Kitty. He said *Mama*, and David never did."

"When he was little," Mama whispered. "He did then. He always said Mama, he had such a sweet way of saying it."

Evie looked at her worriedly. Her mother's eyes looked huge and black, and she was pale. "I'm sure all the things she said were true," she said gently, rubbing Mama's cold hands. "He misses us, and he loves us." *It is true*, she told herself. *He doesn't mind that I didn't say goodbye properly, I know he doesn't.*

"We didn't need her to tell us that," Kitty agreed.

"I only wanted to talk to him one last time. Oh, David!" Mama pulled her hands out of Evie's and pressed them to her mouth. Then she plunged away across the room, and they heard her run sobbing up the stairs.

Chapter Thirteen

Mama didn't talk about communicating with the spirit world any more. She came downstairs the next day with her face pale and swollen with tears, and hardly spoke. The girls' father had just come back exhausted from his shift and the meal was practically silent. Even Max wasn't whining for toast crusts – the spirit hand seemed to have been made of quite old liver, or perhaps Eugenia had been using it for a while. He had been dramatically sick just as Evie was going to bed the night before.

After their father had gone off to sleep for a couple of hours, Evie leaned over to talk to her mother. "Mama . . . it's nearly time for Kitty and me to go to school. Will you be all right? We could stay at home, if it would help."

Kitty looked up eagerly, but Mama shook her head and managed a small smile. "I'm quite all right. I suppose it should be a funny story, shouldn't it? How we were almost taken in by such a dreadful fraud. It's just that I hoped. . ."

"I think that's what she was depending on," Evie said, scowling. "We wanted it to be real so much that we'd have believed anything. It's an awful thing for her to do."

"You ought to give Max a reward," Kitty put in. "If it wasn't for him, we'd still think she was real."

"Yes." Mama looked down at her cup of tea, and for a moment, Evie wished that Eugenia *had* conned them all, and Mama was still floating about in a deluded dream. But she only wished it for a moment.

Mrs Weatherill had clearly spread the story of

what had happened around the old ladies from the church. There was a chorus of disapproving whispers as Evie and Kitty followed Mama and Daddy into their pew that Sunday. Even the girls' father glanced around, confused by the critical twittering of elderly ladies.

"Mrs Weatherill's over there giving us the evil eye," Kitty whispered. "Look. She's got that horrible fox fur tippet on, with the little teeth. Ugh."

"They're all staring at us." Evie glared straight ahead, entirely missing Grace, who was sitting with her parents on the other side of the aisle and trying to signal to her discreetly with a mission pamphlet. "You'd think they'd be grateful to know she made it all up. I bet Eugenia doesn't do séances out of the goodness of her heart, does she? I wonder how much she charges?"

"I should think absolutely tons," Kitty agreed. "But I hope no one says anything to Mama about it in front of Daddy. Since he said she couldn't have a séance and she did anyway."

Evie nodded. Their mother was staring straight ahead just as she was, but there were small red blotches on the tops of her cheeks. She knew perfectly well that they were being whispered about. Evie wondered if she was worried about disobeying their father, and being caught out. But she looked angry rather than worried.

After the service, Evie and Kitty tried to shoo their parents out of the church and home, but there was a crowd around the porch talking to Mr Allen, the vicar, and they couldn't get past.

"Mama, I feel faint," Evie said, noticing that Mrs Weatherill was bearing down on them, with several other ladies close behind. "The church was awfully hot today. Can we please go home?"

"She looks like she's going to be sick," Kitty added, trying to look meaningfully at Mama. But they were too late.

"Mrs Maitland," Mrs Weatherill said coldly, bowing slightly as she sailed past, and the ladies in her wake only managed the very tiniest of bows too. One of them was wearing a distinctly sneering expression.

"Good God, Helen." The girls' father watched them go, and then added in a low voice, "What have you done to offend that gang of old tabbies? I've never seen them look quite so frozen-faced."

Mama smiled faintly and put her arm through his. "I'm sorry, darling. Evie and Max saved me from doing something rather stupid."

Evie looked worriedly at her father. He had flatly forbidden Mama to invite Eugenia to the house – what would he say when he found out she'd done it anyway?

"Do you remember our argument last week, about the spiritualist?" Mama made a little shooing motion with her fingers, telling Evie and Kitty to walk ahead – but they could still hear, and they kept darting looks over their shoulders.

"Of course I do." Their father looked at her and groaned. "Oh, Helen. You didn't?"

"Charlie, I was desperate! Alice Weatherill promised me that the woman would contact David. That I'd be able to speak to him again. I couldn't not. . ."

"But it's rubbish – they're all frauds, Helen, it's an absolute waste of money. These spiritualists are just leeching off people who are suffering – they're criminals!"

"Well, luckily, I didn't get to the stage of giving her any money," Mama said soothingly. "Only – only of believing her, and then being heartbroken when I found out what a fool I was."

"Helen, what happened?" He stopped, taking her hands and looking at her worriedly. "What did she do?"

"She spoke to me as David." Mama's voice was shaking. "She was very clever – but she didn't even need to be. She didn't tell me anything that wasn't common knowledge. The only mistake she made I covered up for her myself, because I wanted to believe so much."

"So what happened to make you see what was going on?"

Mama laughed. "Max. It was awful at the time, but looking back on it, even I have to see that it was funny. She was manifesting a spirit hand."

"A *what*? This sounds like the most beastly nonsense, Helen."

"Yes . . . I can see that now. But it was very real, in the dark, and with the eerie noises she was making. We were all so worked up, and we wanted it to be true."

"We? You mean you subjected the girls to this?" His voice sharpened angrily and Mama flinched. Kitty and Evie stopped pretending they weren't listening and hurried back.

"It was good we were there," Kitty told their father earnestly. "Honestly, Daddy. Mama was so upset, and it's all very well you forbidding her to do things, but she *needed* somebody to talk to."

"Kitty, don't. . ." Mama murmured. "I know,

Charles, I'm sorry. It was stupid – but I was angry. You wouldn't listen, you just thundered away, and truly, it seemed that I had to do it."

He sighed. "I suppose I did storm about as the master of the house a little. So, Evie, what did your horrible hound do?"

"He ate Eugenia's spirit hand – it was sitting on the edge of the table, and he jumped up and stole it. And before you say I ought to train him better, Daddy, I shouldn't think he'll ever do it again, because she'd made it out of terribly off liver, and he was sick for ages after he ate it."

"Liver!" He wrinkled his nose, his moustache quivering, and then burst out laughing. "Serves him right. So why are Mrs Weatherill and that bunch of harpies looking at you as though you aren't nice to know?"

Mama sighed. "Eugenia is Alice's find. She's disgusted with me, because of course she still believes in her absolutely. Or she's telling herself she does."

"Even after the liver?" Their father shook his head, still chuckling. "How's she explaining that away?"

Mama shrugged. "Who knows. But I have a feeling that my coffee morning might be a little thin on the ground. Alice has a long tongue."

Daddy snorted. "Nonsense. Of course people will come – they'll want the gossip. You'll probably raise a fortune."

The year ground on. The winter wasn't nearly as cold as the year before – when David had written to them about trenches full of snow, and made rather miserable jokes about feeling like a polar bear – but it seemed worse, somehow. Evie was sure that it went on being grey and cold and grim for months.

For Evie and Kitty – and possibly for their father too – the winter had begun in November, with a letter from Brandy's keeper.

He is a grand dog, very bright and obedient, and a hard worker as all Airedales seem to be. We have mostly collies, lurchers and Airedales here, and the Airedales take their work seriously. I promise you that he has enjoyed his training, as we are very gentle with them. You see, the dogs must be able to take pride in their work, and truly enjoy it. When Brandy is sent with a message he will be two or three miles away from me, so he must think of me as the source of everything that is pleasant, and want to run back to me as fast as he can.

He was quite nervous of the rifle fire at the start of his training, but now he is an old hand, and minds it less than he would a fly buzzing past his ear. He is positively raring to go, which is good, as we are embarking for France very soon – excuse me if I do not tell you the exact date. I know he will make me very proud, and you too.

Rifle fire! Darling Brandy, forced to listen to guns until he no longer noticed the noise of them. It was horrible. Yet at the same time, reading a letter from the man who would be out there in France with him helped a little. At least they knew that someone was looking after him – someone who thought he was as special and good as they did. Evie knew exactly what Keeper Marsh meant about Brandy taking things seriously. He always had. He thought of all the Maitland children as his special charge, and had followed Alecky everywhere – obviously he understood that Alecky was the one most likely to cause trouble. Even when they went scrambling on the beach, he had hopped around in a constant circle from rock to rock and child to child, trying to make sure that none of them were going to fall. Several times he had hauled Alecky back down from the edge of the cliff, when he thought he was going too far up. Alecky always said Brandy fussed worse than Miss Jennings, but really he had adored him. Evie couldn't decide if it was better that Alecky had never known about Brandy being sent to France or not. He would have been so proud, she thought, but he would probably have missed Brandy even more than she and Kitty did, and felt that as a boy, he mustn't show it.

All through the war, they had celebrated Christmas – not quite as grandly as before, of course. But this year it was harder to find the Christmas spirit. The girls' father took them to the pantomime in Scarborough, but it wasn't the same. Aladdin's cave dripped with sparkling jewels, just like the gorgeous sets Evie remembered from previous years, but the jokes and songs didn't seem as funny. When a troupe of little girls danced on singing "Keep the Home Fires Burning", Evie couldn't bear it any longer. She struggled out of their row, past cross children and more sympathetic mothers, and stood shaking in the corridor outside until the show was over.

"It was a stupid song to sing anyway," Kitty said afterwards in the train home. "Why on earth would they sing that in Arabia, or wherever Aladdin was? I expect they just put it in to make everybody cry. Or it was the only song those girls could sing. Do you want my handkerchief, Evie? Your nose is scarlet."

Evie nodded gratefully. She couldn't work out if she was tearful because of David, or because she kept thinking about Brandy missing his Christmas treats, the new collar and the smidgeon of roast turkey – although this year they were having a decidedly less festive chicken, as turkeys seemed to be in short supply. It might even be that worrying about Brandy made her feel guilty that she wasn't sadder about her brother. She couldn't tell – there seemed to be a hard stone of worry and unhappiness deep in the middle of her, and even presents and the party that she and Kitty went to at Grace's house on Boxing Day couldn't melt it away.

The grey, damp weather carried on and on. Kitty and Evie were struggling back home from school against driving rain one April afternoon when a figure in a yellow oilskin coat met them at the front gate. He half bowed, hunched against the rain, and the girls peered at him under their rain hats.

"Oh! Mr Armstrong." Evie nodded to him politely. "Good afternoon. Have you come to see my father?"

"Yes – I went to the office, but they said he was here. I haven't an appointment. . ."

"I'm sure he won't mind." Evie struggled with the garden gate, her cold fingers slipping on the latch, and it was only when Frank Armstrong tried to help her with it that she realized he had one arm. The other sleeve of his oilskin was flapping loose

Kitty stared at him, and then looked away quickly. They had both taken little presents and knitted things to the convalescent hospital for soldiers, and they had seen men with missing limbs. It felt different in a hospital though – one was prepared when one visited and, besides, the men were strangers. They hadn't known them before, with all limbs intact.

"Last time you saw me, you were kind enough to stand up for me, Miss Kitty," Frank said politely as he followed them up the garden path.

"Oh! The white feathers!" Kitty turned back to stare at him in surprise. "I'd forgotten."

"Well, I remembered. I wished I'd thanked you properly, but I was so embarrassed, all I wanted to do was get away. So, thank you." He gave a strangled sort of laugh. "At least I won't get accused of shirking now, I suppose."

The girls nodded nervously. "I suppose not," Evie said, trying to smile. "But – but I should think you'd still prefer. . ." She stammered to a halt. "Excuse me, I must just unlock the door."

She fought her key into the lock, glad to turn away. She was scarlet with embarrassment. Of course he'd prefer still to have two arms! How could she have said something so stupid?

"I'll go and find Daddy," Kitty said as soon as the door was open, and she dashed away to the study, leaving Evie trying to take Mr Armstrong's coat, and pretending not to notice as he struggled to get himself out of it.

"Not used to this yet," he murmured apologetically.

"Frank!" The girls' father hurried out into the hall, holding his hands to shake Frank's. Then he stopped short. Kitty obviously hadn't had a chance to tell him about Frank's arm. "Good God, I'm so sorry," he murmured.

"Mr Maitland, I just wanted to talk to you about something. Could we, er. . . ?" He waved towards the study door.

"Of course – but Frank, if it's that you'd like your job back, you don't have to ask."

"At the moment the regiment is keeping me on, sir; I'm being moved to a desk job at a training camp. But I had to see you before I went. It's important."

The girls' father nodded and led Frank into his study, closing the door behind them.

Evie and Kitty looked at each in surprise. "I

wonder what's so important?" Evie said. "He had that look – like someone who has to own up to something, and doesn't want to." She sighed. "I should go and start doing my prep. There's loads of it." The work seemed to have doubled now that she was in the Upper Fourth, and her prep always took ages. She was fighting with French composition when Kitty came thundering up the stairs and swung on the doorknob. "Daddy wants us."

"What? Why?" Evie gathered up Max, who was sleeping on her lap, and he groaned and wriggled.

"Don't know. Mama's home from her meeting; he said he has to talk to all of us."

Evie looked worriedly at her French – it wasn't even nearly finished – but followed Kitty downstairs to the parlour. Their father was standing by the fireplace, his arm resting on the mantelpiece. He looked worried, and rather pale. Mama was sitting in an armchair, frowning. "Now, *please*, Charles, tell us what on earth is going on?"

"I wanted the girls to hear this too." He pounded his fist lightly against the mantel, and Evie suddenly remembered watching David thump her bed, the day he told them that war had broken out. He'd had just that same worried, frustrated look – half excited too. "I don't know. . ." Daddy frowned, and hesitated, and then forced the words out. "Frank came to see me because he was part of the same company as David last year. He was there, when – when David was lost. He had only just rejoined the unit, which I suppose is why David hadn't told us in his letters that they'd seen each other."

"We knew they were in the same regiment," Mama said quietly. "Did he tell you what happened, Charles? We never knew exactly, the letter from his commanding officer was so vague."

The girls' father spun away from the fireplace and crouched down beside her, taking her hand. Evie jumped as Kitty's cold fingers gripped hers.

"Helen, he told me that he thinks David is still alive."

Mama stared at him, and shook her head slightly.

"Yes." Their father went on, his voice trembling a little. "Frank was injured in the same attack, it's where he lost his arm. Poor chap was desperately unlucky, he'd hardly recovered from his previous injury. This time he was sent to a convalescent hospital to get better. He had head injuries as well, so he's only just come back from the hospital. No one had told him that David was dead."

"If he's not dead," Kitty faltered, "then where is he?" She looked around, as if she expected their brother to appear from behind the sofa.

"Frank says he's *certain* that David was alive. He says he spoke to him, that he was injured but definitely alive. But he thinks David was taken prisoner – there was a party of German soldiers out looking for casualties, and he swears he saw them pick David up." He sighed. "This is – this is the problem. They didn't take Frank, because he was half unconscious. They either didn't see him at all, or they thought he was already dead. Which means he could have imagined all this in a state of delirium. He admitted as much to me, that he had quite severe head injuries. But he says he's sure, as sure as he can be. Mind you, it's not far off a year since we were told Davy had died. Ten months, I suppose." He stopped, and took in a shuddering breath. "So it seems to me that if he were alive, we would have heard by now. Somehow. The whole thing is very – uncertain."

"David isn't dead." Mama stared at Daddy, but Evie wasn't sure she was seeing him. Her own heart was suddenly beating so fast that she felt dizzy.

"Charles, if this is some cruel trick. . ." Mama whispered.

"It isn't. That I'm sure of. Frank truly believes that David is a prisoner of war. But there's no proof, and even though he believes it, he may still simply be wrong. Or David may have died since he was captured. I wasn't even sure whether to tell you all, whether I would only be causing you more pain. Then I thought about that godforsaken séance, and decided I must." He clutched Mama's hand tighter, and turned to look at Evie and Kitty. "No more secrets."

Chapter Fourteen

For the next few weeks everyone in the house seemed to be balanced on some sort of seesaw. There were moments of intense, hopeful happiness, when Mama kissed Mrs Dixon on the cheek in the middle of a conversation about jam tarts, because they were David's favourite. But they were balanced with deep depressions. Kitty and Evie both kept creeping into David's room – which was just as it had always been, because no one had been able to bear the thought of tidying it. Drifts of paper scrawled with drawings, broken bits of pencil, dried-up tubes of paint, all stacked on every surface. It even still smelled of paint and linseed oil. They stood there, breathing it in, wondering if he would really be coming back. Or was it all just a fantastical story that Frank had dreamed up when he was half-dead himself?

Even if David did come back, Evie wondered to herself as she wrestled a squashed tube of paint out of Max's mouth, what would he be like? What would he think of her? She had been so cold and unsympathetic when he'd tried to tell her what was really happening out there. She had run away, because she couldn't bear to have her tall, handsome brother telling her how scared he was. Now, surely, he would be feeling even worse – he had been blown up and captured, and he was being subjected to who knew what sort of brutality in a prison camp. Had he spent all that time remembering that she had been too angry to say goodbye?

The common-sense side of Evie tried to tell the

rest of her that it had probably been the last thing on his mind, but it didn't stop her brooding over it. At least if he really was alive – *if* – she would have the chance to tell him she was sorry.

Their father had responded to the news by hurling himself into action. He had written to the Army Office, to their MP, to the Red Cross, to everyone who might have some tiny particle of influence, begging for news. He had even written to the king, pointing out that David was not that different in age to his own son Prince Albert, who had been serving in the Royal Navy. He asked for the king's help in finding out what had happened, although he did admit that he wasn't really expecting an answer to that one. Several weeks afterwards, he did receive a beautifully written note from one of the king's secretaries, saying that they had passed the letter on through the correct channels, and assuring them of His Majesty's deepest sympathy in this difficult time. It wasn't particularly helpful.

Then, at last, a packet of letters came, forwarded by the Red Cross. No one was quite sure if they'd just happened to turn up, or if it was Mr Maitland's letters that had made a difference. They were very tattered, and written with a bad pen. The mixture of splodges and spidery writing made them hard to read. There were tiny drawings crammed around the words – portraits, little cartoons of strutting guards, and their own faces, odd memories of home between the lines.

12 November 1917

Dear all,

I'm not sure whether this letter will even reach you. We are supposed to be able to write two letters a month (so please forgive me for lumping all of you together), but the others tell me that very regularly the director or one of the camp officers will decide to withdraw the privilege for some imagined crime. I'm going to write anyway, as at least then I can imagine you reading this. To bc perfectly honest, there isn't much else to do. A very musical chap is trying to arrange a concert – we are in the most derelict tumbledown old barracks of a castle, and there is a piano, although it has a mouse's nest in it. Unfortunately the only songs anyone seems to know are extremely rude, and he's got a bit disheartened about the whole thing.

I suppose I should begin at the beginning and carry on until I get to the end, but it's very difficult to do without getting led astray. I have been here two days now, after being transferred from hospital. I was caught in a shell blast, as far as I can remember, and must have spent a long time drifting in and out of consciousness. I came to in hospital, a German Lazarett, which was a rather horrible shock, though in fact they were remarkably kind to the enemy, and we were quite well-looked-after. I hadn't expected this, after all the stories in the papers about Hun brutality, and German soldiers finishing off the wounded on the battlefield. But I suppose one cannot expect an entire nation to have gone utterly bad, after all.

But the place I'm in now, sadly, is doing its best to live up to all the rumours. Endless, pettifogging rules, and a deep delight in catching us breaking them. (Reminds me of school, actually.) The guards themselves aren't too bad, pleasant old chaps, most of them, but the director and the officers are a nasty lot. The food is rather dreadful (though better than in the soldiers' camp, poor devils), but we seem to get lucky with the Red Cross parcels, so we live mostly on biscuits.

I suppose you will want to know what sort of a state I'm in. All limbs present and correct, but I now come with added shrapnel in my right shoulder, though I'm told it's not actually doing me any harm. It's mostly healed, but it took a while and got infected and the swelling made it rather difficult to write to you before now. The main damage was from the blast – I was thrown a considerable distance, literally knocked sideways, and deafened. My hearing is still a bit dodgy, but gradually getting better, I think. I seem to have lost a great deal of time where I wasn't quite sure who I was or what I was doing, but I count myself incredibly lucky.

Write back to me, won't you? The others assure me that we do receive letters, though often none for weeks and then a great bundle.

All my love,

David

No one knew quite what had happened to the letters. It was obvious that David had known after the first couple that they weren't getting through, but he had kept writing anyway. There were ten of them, so his ration of two a month, but with several gaps when the camp officers had clamped down. The later ones were rather rambling, and more like a diary than letters that actually expected an answer.

They had been forwarded on by the Red Cross, and the covering note said apologetically that no one was quite sure what had happened – that a great cache of letters from that camp had suddenly appeared, not only Lieutenant Maitland's. Perhaps the camp officers had just not bothered to send them on, or they had been forgotten... The Red Cross official promised to do her absolute utmost to get any replies to Lieutenant Maitland as quickly as possible.

They wrote. Letters and letters, apologizing, explaining, begging for replies. Trying to answer his months of weary questions all at once, and tell him everything that had happened. Evie sent him pages describing the séance – then she dithered about sending it, in case he felt odd about having been presumed dead, but in the end she decided he would find it funny.

9 July 1918
Dearest David,

   I expect you are getting a bit bored with all
the letters now. If you are actually getting them,
of course. I wonder if they'll all come at the

same time, like yours. I hope the parcels Mama is sending will arrive soon too. Mrs Dixon was horrified to hear that you were eating mostly biscuits and she has made an enormous and very solid fruit cake. Hopefully the post office won't decide that it's too heavy to send. I hadn't realized how lucky we were when you were in France, to have the letters back from you so regularly. I hope that awful Goldteeth and Beerbreath haven't decided to take away the mail again. Your story about them throwing letters on a bonfire in front of all those desperate prisoners was heartbreaking. Oh, it's so odd to write this and not know whether it will get to you! I can't imagine how you went on writing so diligently for months and months with no reply.

I'm trying to think of anything exciting to tell you, but I think I put it all in the letter I wrote yesterday. We are studying algebra, and I really can't see the use of it at all. At least those silly word problems about building walls or doing the shopping might help us one day, but really, who actually cares about the value of x? Mind you, Kitty seems to love maths all of a sudden, and apparently she is desperate to win her form prize. Miss Lovelock has told her she has a gift, or so Kitty says, but I'm inclined to think she's making it up.

Poor Max still isn't eating properly, and I think it must be the heat, it's been so hot and sunny here. He just seems to lie around dolefully with his chin on his paws, and he turns down even the nicest food, like the sausage I sneaked him from breakfast. (It was my only one as well.) Daddy thinks that he's worrying about you – he says that dogs are very clever, and can sense these things, but I don't think that makes sense at all. Why would he be more upset about you being a prisoner than he was when you were dead? Because I'm sorry to say he didn't seem the slightest bit bothered then. Unless, I suppose, he knew that you weren't? But you were injured,

and unconscious down the side of a shell hole,
so I think that should have been worth his dog
instincts being worried about. I'm actually hoping
that the sunny weather breaks soon, and then he
starts to feel better.

With much love,

Evie

8 July 1918

Dear Miss Maitland,

Many thanks for your letter from June, and
the cigarettes. I do appreciate your sending them.
Miss Maitland, I am very sorry to tell you that I
have bad news about Brandy. It pains me to write
that he was killed by a sniper yesterday evening
while delivering a message. He has worked so
hard and so earnestly, you should have a great deal
of pride in his service. A few days ago he brought
a vital message from the battalion he was with,
that they were cut off under a heavy barrage and
desperately in need of help. It was due to Brandy

that reinforcements were sent to them, and a great many men saved. I tell you this so that you may understand what a good, clever dog he has been.

Regretfully I remain yours,

Keeper Thomas Marsh

It was the wrong letter. Evie stood in the hallway, her hands shaking as she scanned through the lines again, willing the words to reshape themselves, to mean something else. They had been looking out for letters so hopefully, snatching them up as soon they came through the letter box. It made this one seem particularly cruel. It should have been a reply from David. They deserved good news, it was almost *promised*.

Evie went back to the beginning of the letter again, noticing that Brandy's keeper sounded really quite miserable.

She could hear Mama in the parlour, calling to her, asking if it was a letter from David, but she didn't answer. Instead she sat down on the bottom step of the stairs, and Max crawled sadly into her lap. She could see the bumps along his spine – he wasn't as padded and shiny as he had been a few days before.

"How did you know?" she asked him, trying to count back. When exactly had he stopped eating? It wasn't a coincidence, she was sure.

Max only whined, and tried to bury his nose inside the crook of her arm. Evie huddled over him lovingly. "I suppose you thought he was going to come back," she whispered. "I'm sorry."

Chapter Fifteen

They were supposed to be happy, that was the awful thing. Everyone who came to the house, everyone at school, even acquaintances they met in the street wanted to tell them how incredibly lucky they were.

Kitty gloried in the drama of it, and entertained her friends with snippets from David's letters. It was grand, to be the sister of a miracle, especially when the story was written up in the local paper. Evie grew so tired of smiling and saying, "Yes, isn't it wonderful?" It *was* wonderful, she knew it was, and she was happy, of course. It was just that underneath the happiness, she kept thinking of Brandy, and wondering if it had hurt. Not that he would have complained. He hadn't made a fuss at all about that boy hitting him with a rock four years before.

Had they buried him? Keeper Marsh hadn't said in the letter, and she had a horrible feeling that burial for dogs might not be very important, not when sometimes they couldn't even bury the soldiers properly. But the thought of him lying where he had fallen, or thrown on a pile of rubbish, when he had tried so hard and been so good, made her feel sick.

Max gradually began to eat again, but he seemed to have lost some of his cheerful bounciness. Every so often when they were out walking he would see another dog in the distance, and his whole body would quiver. Every inch of him was suddenly alive, watching, listening, sniffing – until the other dog came close enough for him to see that it wasn't Brandy after all, and he sagged.

When Brandy had first been sent away, Evie had found one of his old collars on a toy dog in the nursery, and she had tucked it away in a drawer in her room. Now she hung it over the wooden post at the end of her bed, where she could see it as she lay in bed at night. Max slept curled between the bedpost and Evie's feet, as if he were guarding them both.

The drama of David's miraculous reappearance led the town gossip for weeks, but then it became gradually overshadowed by the war news. The Allies were advancing, and the Germans had withdrawn to the Hindenburg Line. The atmosphere was cautiously hopeful – it began to feel as if this was the beginning of the end. But the optimism was undermined by the creeping threat of illness. A new disease seemed to be sweeping across the country, or further. Even soldiers at the front were catching it. It stole away the strong, and the healthy, and it was so frighteningly fast. The little ones at school had picked up a new skipping rhyme. Miss Boyd banned it after a week, saying that it was distasteful, but it was too catchy to forget.

> *I had a little bird,*
> *Its name was Enza*
> *I opened the window,*
> *And influenza.*

There had been a few cases of the flu earlier in the year, mostly confined to older people, or those already fragile, but now it was back, and it was everywhere.

One of the ladies from church came calling in a state of doleful excitement, to tell Mama that the vicar had been taken suddenly sick with the influenza the day before.

"Dear Mr Allen! Oh, how dreadful," Mama murmured, as Miss Bishop gazed across the tea table, her eyes wide and dramatic behind her glasses. "His poor wife. I suppose we should call, although I wouldn't want to bother her, if she's busy nursing him. Perhaps we could just leave some fruit. Or some little biscuits, Mr Allen might like those as he's recovering."

Evie frowned. She could just imagine what Sarah and Mrs Dixon would say about that. Butter and sugar had been rationed since the summer. The rationing had actually been a relief, since it meant some of the queues were shorter. But Mrs Dixon was not going to be happy wasting her hard-won sugar on the vicar. She always complained that his sermons were too long, and they interfered with the serving of Sunday dinner.

Miss Bishop shook her head and leaned across the table. "My dear Mrs Maitland, you don't understand – I didn't make myself clear, I'm so sorry. . ."

She didn't look in the slightest bit sorry, Evie thought. She looked as though she was positively adoring this. Her eyes glinted, and her voice dropped to a hushed whisper. "Mr Allen has *passed*."

"But – but I thought you said he was only taken ill yesterday," Mama exclaimed, and Kitty's mouth fell open.

"He's dead?" Evie stared at Miss Bishop, who nodded, her eyes flicking from Mama to Evie to Kitty and back again, enjoying their surprise.

"Isn't it awful? So sudden. This dreadful influenza." She gathered up her bag, and nodded to Mama. "I'm so sorry, dear Mrs Maitland, I must be going. I hate to break up our little tea party, but the afternoon is just running away with me."

"She means that she wants to rush off and be first with the gossip somewhere else," Evie said, as she came back from seeing Miss Bishop out.

"Evie..." Mama murmured, but she didn't sound as though she really disapproved. "I just can't believe it."

Kitty giggled. "I expect Mrs Weatherill's setting up a séance this very minute."

"Oh, Kitty! Even Alice Weatherill wouldn't.

Well – I suppose she might. . . Kitty, how can you, when poor Mr Allen has just died. . ."

But even Mama had to put her hand to her mouth to hide a smile.

The armistice almost went unnoticed in the Maitland house. Evie was honestly too busy to think about it a great deal. Everyone except her and Mrs Dixon was laid low with the influenza, and Evie felt as though she had been nursing her family for weeks. Her father had caught it first, hauling himself home from a night shift in the second week of November and practically collapsing on the doorstep. He had been helping to watch for ships from the cliffs, and he was chilled to the bone and couldn't stop shivering. Later the same day, a tray of tea slid out of Sarah's hands and crashed to the floor, and Mama sent her to bed at once. Sarah didn't even argue, just let Evie and Kitty drag her upstairs to her attic room, though she did draw the line at letting them help her undress.

Kitty was next, crying for Evie and Mama in the night. When Evie went to her, she found her turning from side to side in her bed, whimpering that she was too hot, and her pillow was rough, and she didn't like it. She wanted Mama, and Evie was to fetch her, now, *now*! She was wailing, and Max, who'd jumped off Evie's bed and followed her in case it was breakfast, began to whine.

Kitty's cheeks were flushed and burning, but it was her eyes that scared Evie most. They used oil lamps up on the nursery floor, as there was no gas installed, and the soft light from the lamp caught in Kitty's grey eyes, so they shone silvery like mirrors. Alecky's eyes had looked like that, as if he was looking at something very far away. Evie remembered hating it. She stood hesitating, wanting to run for Mama, but reluctant to leave Kitty in that strange state. Then Kitty blinked, and yawned, and seemed to be back in the room with her.

"I want Brandy," Kitty whispered. "Evie, where

is he? I want him to sleep on my bed, my feet are so cold. Can't you get him? Mama won't mind this once."

Evie swallowed and shook her head, setting the lamp down on the bedside table. "I can't, Kitty darling. He's – he's been out in the garden and he's covered in mud. He can't go on your bed, what would Sarah say?"

Kitty only whimpered, but she seemed to accept that this made sense. She nodded, and clawed miserably at the blankets until Evie spread them over her again, smoothing them around her and tucking her in. "Look, I'll put Max by your feet," Evie murmured, lifting him up and hoping that the little dog would stay. He gazed at her, obviously confused – he never slept on Kitty's bed, always on Evie's – but she whispered, "Stay, Maxie," and he snuffled a little, and slumped down over the tiny lump under the quilt that was Kitty's feet.

"You found Brandy!" Kitty whispered. She sighed, and curled herself into her pillow, closing her eyes. Max looked up at Evie, his black eyes knowing and worried, and Evie sat down at the end of the bed next to him, pulling Kitty's shawl around her shoulders, and watched her little sister sleep.

Mama woke them the next morning, wrapped in a dressing gown, her hair unbrushed and straggling down her back. "Evie," she murmured. "Darling, I'm so sorry."

Evie blinked up at her. "I think Kitty has the influenza too," she muttered hoarsely, still half asleep.

"Evie, I feel dreadfully strange." Mama clutched the end of Kitty's bed. "Everything's spinning."

Evie gazed at her, suddenly wide awake. Daddy. Sarah. Kitty. And now Mama.

"I think you should go back to bed," she murmured, wriggling out of the tangled nest of blankets. Max popped his head up curiously, like a snake out of a basket, and Mama stared at him, as if she couldn't quite place what he was.

"Yes," she murmured. "But Daddy, and Kitty. . . And you won't have Sarah."

"I know. Mama, should I call Dr Hargreaves?"

"Mama!" Kitty woke, and blinked at her. "Mama, I don't feel well."

"I know, darling." Mama sat down on Kitty's bed, and stroked her hair. Then she closed her eyes, and her face seemed to sag. Evie eyed them, chewing her lip. Wouldn't it be easier if they were both in the same place? She pulled the blankets around her mother, and gently lifted her feet up – they were quite bare. She couldn't remember when she had last seen Mama's feet.

"Stay, Max. Look after them," she murmured to him. When she looked back from the door, Mama and Kitty were asleep, with Kitty slumped against Mama's shoulder. Max was sitting watchfully by their feet.

Afterwards, Evie heard stories about the worst cases of influenza, cases like Mr Allen, where the body fought the disease so violently that the skin turned bluish-purple, and blood trickled from the patient's nose and ears. She realized that she and her family had been lucky, although they didn't feel that way at the time. As the maroons were fired from the cliffs to celebrate the end of four years of war, she listened to Mama and Kitty coughing and coughing, snatching a breath, only to be doubled over with coughing again. It was Sarah who was worst hit, though, lying quietly at the end of the passage, feebly protesting when Evie brought her tea, or soup. She didn't even cough, just lay, too weak to move.

Evie had to leave helping Sarah drink a cup of tea to dash down the stairs and answer the door to the girl bringing the telegram. Then she sidled into the kitchen holding it, to consult with Mrs Dixon.

"It's addressed to Daddy," she said, holding it out.

"What're you doing with it down here then?"

Mrs Dixon snapped. She was chopping vegetables for yet another pan of soup, and she looked exhausted. She had told Evie the day before that she quite fancied getting that flu herself for a bit of a rest. Then she'd sat down heavily at the kitchen table, and put her face in her hands. "I shouldna said that, Miss Evie. I'm only tired."

"What if it's bad?" Evie asked now. "He's up today, he's sitting in the armchair in his study. I made him a fire in there. But if this is about David." She gripped the envelope tighter. "It might make him worse again. He could have a relapse."

Mrs Dixon frowned, and eyed the telegram. "Tha could open it, and see."

They stared at each other, and Evie shook her head. "Then I'd have to tell him," she whispered.

Her father was sitting by the window in his study, with the newspaper spread over his lap, but he wasn't reading it. He was staring vaguely out of the window, but his face sharpened as Evie handed him the telegram. The bones were there, under his skin, and Evie wished she hadn't had to show him. He tore it open, his fingers shaking so much that the envelope ripped right across.

"Good God." He shook his head and slumped back in the chair.

"I shouldn't have brought it to you," Evie said miserably. "I'm sorry, Daddy. Is it David? Is he dead after all, in the camp?" She came closer, both wanting and not wanting to look.

"Dead?" Her father started to laugh, and then to cough. He waved away the water Evie tried to hand him, and sat panting for a moment. "Ha! Evie – he's in London!" He waved the telegram at her.

"What?" Evie snatched it out of his hand.

Arrived London yesterday. Meet train Whitby 4.15. Much love David.

"I must get properly dressed," Evie's father muttered, flapping at his dressing gown.

"You can't go! I mean, I'm sorry, Daddy. But you can't. It took you twenty minutes to get down the stairs."

"Someone has to meet him, Evie. He's been in prison for over a year. We can't leave him standing at the station."

"I'll go."

Her father eyed her doubtfully. "On your own? That doesn't seem—"

"Daddy, it's 1918. Girls not much older than me have spent the last four years driving ambulances, and making bombs. I can walk to the station." Evie caught her breath, hoping that he was too exhausted to shout at her. She never normally spoke to him that way – she hadn't raised her voice to him since their dreadful fight about Brandy. "I'll take Max," she added shakily.

But he only sighed, the sudden flare of excitement draining to leave him pale again. "Yes. You've been very good, Evie, looking after us all. Tell your mother, won't you?" He looked again at the telegram and said shakily, "You're quite right. I can't even face walking up the stairs to find her."

Evie had hardly needed to go to Whitby Station since they had sent Brandy away. There had been no visits to their aunt in London, or their grandparents, since everyone was so busy with war work – fundraising, or running refreshment stands for troop trains, or helping in hospitals. So as she waited on the platform, she had to look across the tracks to where they'd stood the year before, holding Brandy's lead with her hand over Kitty's. Her ears filled with that thin, high wail that was Brandy and Kitty together as the train began to move.

But it wasn't Brandy whose lead she was holding, and the wail was the whistle of an approaching train. Max tugged anxiously, pulling away from the edge, unsettled by the growing noise. Evie picked him up and stroked him, moving back to stand out of the way as porters appeared, and the stationmaster. The train hissed into the station, billowing steam, and Max wriggled in her arms. He was braver now that he was being held, and he barked at the train, his tail beating against her coat. Evie shushed him, worried that he might leap down and get under everyone's feet, and she didn't see David step out of the train and walk along the platform. Or at least, she did, but she was distracted, and she was looking for a boy in uniform, not a tall, thin man in an ill-fitting suit.

She didn't realize until he was standing in front of her, smiling at her hesitantly, and looking so like Daddy.

Max barked at him, and Evie was so outraged that this was his welcome that she forgot to worry about that last goodbye. She just hugged him, so that they were wrapped together around the frantically squirming dog, and her brother began to laugh.

"I'm not sure he wants me back."

"Oh, he does, he does!" Evie let go, looking up at him. She was silent for a moment, and then she smiled at him shyly. "I can't believe you're here."

"Nor can I. I seem to have been on trains for a very long time." He glanced around, obviously looking for the rest of the family, and Evie hurried to explain.

"They wanted to come. I left Kitty crying because she couldn't – everyone's had flu except for me and Mrs Dixon. Daddy's got as far as coming downstairs in a dressing gown, but Mama and Kitty and Sarah can't get out of bed. Mrs Dixon is thumping around the kitchen trying to make you a special welcome home dinner, but most of the meat ration's gone on beef tea. I'm sure she'll still manage something wonderful, though."

"Are they all right?" David asked worriedly. "It went through the camp, it was horrific, though it seemed to hit the guards harder than us."

"You had it? You didn't put that in your letters," Evie said, surprised.

"No. . ." He shrugged a little. "Did you write to me this week?"

"Well, yes, but it was more of a note, I didn't

have time. . ." Evie trailed off apologetically.

"I didn't mean that – I meant, did you tell me that the whole family had the Spanish flu and you were run ragged trying to look after everyone?"

Evie smiled. "No. Just that Mama wasn't very well and not to expect a letter from her. She did try, but you wouldn't have made head or tail of it. No, you're right, of course. I didn't want to upset you either." She took his arm, and they walked along the platform, and out on to the street. "I'm sorry that you had to be worried about us," she said quietly. "It shouldn't have been that way round. I ought to have listened to you properly, when you tried to tell me what it was like."

David shook his head. "I should never have said it to you, Evie. I cursed myself for it, afterwards. You were a little girl, I was talking about bones falling out of trench walls. I shouldn't—"

"I'm only four years younger than you, and you were there, seeing them!" Evie stopped, pulling him to face her. "I was so angry and upset about

Brandy, I couldn't bear to listen. I wasn't fair."

They walked on through the town in silence, watching Max dance about in front of them, and then David said, "I wish I'd never found him, you know. You were right, it was nothing to do with the poor old chap. Maybe they'll send him back too, now it's over. I should hope so."

"But he's dead," Evie said stupidly. Then she looked up, blinking back tears. "Oh. We didn't tell you that, either."

The house settled back into a strange sort of normality. David retreated to his attic again, and came down for meals, and made polite conversation. In between, he was painting, fiercely determined to go to art school the next year, despite the scarring that had weakened his arm. He had argued about it with their father, but in the end it hadn't been much of a fight. Mr Maitland had always declared that David ought to go to university and study law. He wanted him to join the family firm. But now, when so few young men had come back at all, he was simply grateful that David was there. Instead of referring to his son's paintings as *those daubs of yours* he asked to see them, and made David tear two sketches out so he could prop them on his mantelpiece.

Even so, no one went up to the attic any more. Evie tried, creeping up the stairs the way she always used to, but David met her at the door and gently asked her to go away. There were some things he didn't want her to see.

"I wouldn't mind. Even if it's horrible things," she said, twisting her fingers together. "Why should you have to remember them all on your own?"

He shook his head. "No. Not yet, anyway. I'm not ready to show anyone, Evie, it's not that it's you." Then he smiled at her. "But I have made you something. Stay there a minute." He disappeared into the attic and came back with a long parcel, wrapped up in a bit of old dust sheet. "This is for you. Come outside into the garden with me for a bit." He led her down the stairs, carrying the swathed bundle, while Evie peered at it over his shoulder, trying to work out what it could be. It was quite big, and she had no idea.

They slipped out of the front door and down the steps, and peered across the garden, dank and misty. David made a face. "We should have stopped to fetch coats. Or waited for a better day. Sorry."

"I don't mind." Evie hugged her arms around herself and followed him across the grass to the bench under the tree. She sat down, thinking of the bracelet she'd buried in the grass. She had dug it up again, slipping out that day they'd heard that David was dead, but she could still see the mark in the grass where it had been.

"I thought it could go here," David muttered, placing the bundle on her lap. "It was his favourite place to sit, wasn't it?"

Evie started to unwrap the cloth, and a

square nose appeared, and pricked-up ears. He was looking at her with that slightly worried expression, the face of a dog with a family to watch over. The tight ripples of his fur stood out of the wood, and he was perfect.

"He's not absolutely full-size, of course." David eyed her anxiously. "I couldn't get a piece big enough. But the colours are right. I think so, anyway."

"He's beautiful. It's just like him, you're so clever." Evie crouched down, and set the painted carving next to the bench, so that Brandy was looking out on his garden again.

There was a scuffling of paws, and Max came swinging along the path to find her. Evie glanced at the statue, wondering how he would react, whether he would understand that it was meant to be Brandy. He came up to her, wagging his tail and sniffing lovingly round her feet. Then he jumped up, so that his damp paws were on her knees, heavy and cold through the cloth of her skirt. He didn't seem to notice the statue, until he leaned over and sniffed at its ears, and sneezed.

"Probably the varnish smells odd," David suggested, seeing her sigh.

"I know. I just thought it was so like him, I hoped Max would see it too. But you're right, I expect he's going by the smell." She stood up, and leaned her face against his painty jumper. "It's the most beautiful thing."

The paint faded a little in the winter rain, and Evie brought the statue inside when it snowed, and put him in the nursery. Brandy had liked snow, to run about in and bark at for a little while, but he never stayed out in it for long, and she hated the thought of him being cold.

When the spring came, and the sun grew warmer towards the end of March the next year, she set him out again, and the grass grew up around him so that he looked as though he belonged. Max lay in the sunny patch, just where Brandy always had, stretched out on his back with his paws in the air, and the pink of his stomach showing. Often he lay just in front of the statue, so that one of his soft ears draped over the wooden paws as he slept in the sun.

"He does know it's Brandy, don't you think?" Evie asked, smiling fondly as Max's stomach heaved gently in and out. She was stretched on a rug with Kitty beside her, both of them eating strawberries out of a colander. Daddy hadn't dug up the vegetable patch, but he was growing strawberries, and they had planted asparagus, because it took three years to grow. They could afford to wait that long now, he said.

Kitty looked over at Max and nodded. "I don't think he can be comfortable, squashed up against the statue like that. Brandy's paws are digging into him. He has to be sleeping that way for a reason. He likes being next to him."

David didn't say anything, but he was drawing Kitty and the strawberries, and Evie supposed he just wasn't listening.

Kitty blinked, and yawned. "Mama's calling," she sighed. "We'd better go in."

"Are you coming?" Evie asked David as she folded up the rug, and he grunted something that was probably, "In a minute."

Evie was most of the way down the side passage to the kitchen door when she realized she had abandoned the colander in the long grass, and Mrs Dixon would be wanting it back. She piled the rug by the doorstep and went back out into the garden. Max padded after her a couple of steps, and then gave up and sat down on the folded rug.

She hadn't meant to creep up on her brother, but she had soft shoes on, and the grass muffled her steps. She stood and watched him take a biscuit out of his pocket and crumble it in the grass around the wooden dog's paws.

"What are you doing?" she asked him, puzzled, as she stooped to pick up the colander, and he straightened up sharply and stared at her.

"Nothing!" He put his hands behind his back.

"Were you feeding him?" Evie frowned. "Why would you. . . Oh."

David glanced sideways at the statue, looking a little shifty.

"Is that why Max likes to sleep there now? Because you leave him treats?"

Her brother gave an apologetic little shrug. "You wanted him to. You wanted him to be missing Brandy, and I thought perhaps if I fed him here. . ."

"How long have you been doing that?" Evie demanded crossly.

"Well, since you put the statue back out here. A few months."

"Every day?" Evie asked, disbelievingly.

"Yes. A biscuit, or a bit of cheese. He likes cheese."

"I know." Evie sat down on the bench and looked up at him. "I didn't mind that Max had forgotten. Actually, I don't think he has. It's just that he remembers in a different way. Sometimes he still stops and looks for Brandy when we walk along the cliff path. But only for a moment, and then he goes on again."

Max came pattering over the grass towards them, clearly tired of waiting. He gazed up at Evie, then he twitched his ears and began to snuffle around Brandy's paws for the biscuit, delicately searching out every crumb.

David held out the last piece of biscuit to Evie, and she crouched down and put it just between Brandy's outstretched front paws, and then stroked his wooden nose. Max bustled around the front of the statue again and gulped it down. He did one last circuit, to make sure he hadn't missed any, and gave Evie and David an enquiring look, as if he wondered why they were watching him. Then he barked sharply, and led the way back into the house.

Author's Note

Parts of this story are true, and parts of it very much aren't. Weaving the truth and the story together has been fascinating.

The County School in Whitby really existed, and it's now part of Caedmon College – until very recently, the school even had the piece of shrapnel that fell on the playing field on December 16 1914, narrowly missing a group of children. Karen Purvis at Caedmon College took the time to show me so many fantastic maps, school magazines and photographs – it's thanks to her that the part of the book based at the school came together.

I begged my mother to come on that research trip with me (in December, in the cold) as she was born in Saltburn, not far from Whitby, and knows the town. She put up with me wandering about, taking random photos of useful-looking houses and accidentally menacing a sheep on the cliff path to Saltwick Nab. Thank you for all the books and maps, and answering all my silly questions!

Another thank you to Fiz Osborne and Lauren Fortune, for pointing me towards the story of the raid on Whitby in the first place. (I will write that ghost story I was vaguely planning one of these days!)

The War Dog School was real too, and its founder, Lieutenant Colonel Edwin Richardson, wrote a book about it, *British War Dogs, Their Training and Psychology*. This is the book's dedication:

This book is dedicated to the brave
Dogs of Britain who helped their
country in her hour of need.
FAITHFUL UNTO DEATH

More from Holly Webb

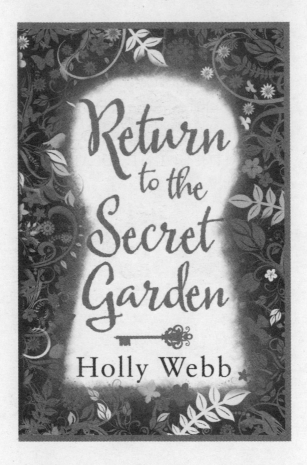

A magical sequel to Frances Hodgson Burnett's
timeless classic *The Secret Garden*